The Journey of Daria

Published by Fideon Press

First Edition

ISBN: 978-1-968169-00-8

Dedication

To my daughter Adelina-Camelia, who reminds me daily that gentleness is strength, and dreams have no expiration date.

"She didn't rise from the ashes. She gathered them—feather by feather—and remembered how to fly."

LOVE, MOM

Table of Contents

The Journal of Daria..

Dedication...

Introduction...

Chapter 1: The Whispering Beginning.....................1

Journal Entry 1: For Her Eyes Only..........................4

Chapter 2: A Familiar Song......................................6

Journal Entry 2: For Her Eyes Only..........................9

Chapter 3: The Unnamed Shadow...........................11

Journal Entry 3: For Her Eyes Only..........................14

Chapter 4: The Dream Beneath the Leaves.............16

Journal Entry 4: For Her Eyes Only..........................19

Chapter 5: The First Word......................................21

Journal Entry 5: For Her Eyes Only..........................24

Chapter 6: Echoes of Lavender.............................26

Journal Entry 6: For Her Eyes Only..........................29

Chapter 7: The Release..31

Journal Entry 7: For Her Eyes Only..........................35

Chapter 8: Where Silence Blooms..........................37

Journal Entry 8: For Her Eyes Only........................40

Chapter 9: The Stranger with Quiet Eyes...............42

Journal Entry 9: For Her Eyes Only.......................45

Chapter 10: The Voice Beneath the Willow............47

Journal Entry 10: For Her Eyes Only......................53

Chapter 11: The Return of the Raven....................55

Journal Entry 11: For Her Eyes Only.....................58

Chapter 12: The Village beneath the Willow...........60

Journal Entry 12: For Her Eyes Only.....................63

Chapter 13: The First Time I Spoke........................66

Journal Entry 13: For Her Eyes Only.....................70

Chapter 14: The Thread between Us.......................73

Journal Entry 14: For Her Eyes Only.....................82

Chapter 15: The Echoes She Carried......................85

Journal Entry 15: For Her Eyes Only.....................93

Chapter 16: The Weight of Becoming Light............96

Journal Entry 16: For Her Eyes Only.....................99

Chapter 17: The Weight of Becoming Light.........102

Journal Entry 17: For Her Eyes Only...............110

PART II.................RETURN..................117

Chapter 18: The Call Home.......................118

Chapter 19: The Echoes Within.....................125

Chapter 20: The Return.............................134

Chapter 21: The First Day of the After.............146

Epilogue – The Quiet After the Echo........................154

Daria's Full Journal...156

About the Author..158

Your own journal.......................................160

Introduction

There is a girl inside each woman, waiting. Not for permission, but for remembrance.

This is not a fairytale. This is a return.

A return to the softness of the world made you hide. A return to the breath you held too long. A return to the voice that once cracked—and now sings.

The Journey of Daria came to me in pieces, like feathers in the wind. I did not set out to write a book. I set out to listen. To the quiet. To the ache. To the voices of women who had forgotten how to speak softly to themselves.

Then… she came to me. A character, yes. But also, a soul.

"My name is Daria," she said. "I once believed I was too broken to begin again. However, something soft and strong called me back— a feather. A breath. A voice."

Daria became the mirror I held to my own story. And the story so many of us carry, quietly, deeply, and bravely.

Therefore, if you are here to remember who you are, you are in the right place. This is your return.

Not with perfection. But with presence. Feather by feather.

Walk with us. Not because we know the destination, but because you were never meant to walk alone.

Chapter 1: The Whispering Beginning

Daria stood beneath the willow tree, where the world seemed to hold its breath. The morning air was cool against her skin, still wet from the kiss of dawn. The long green strands of the willow hung like curtains, swaying gently in rhythm with a wind that spoke in hushed tones. She reached out, letting the silken leaves slide across her fingertips—soft, almost shy, like a secret waiting to be told.

This tree had always known her better than anyone else. It never asked questions. It never interrupted. It simply stood still… and listened.

She had first come here as a child, barefoot and cautious, pulled by something she could not name. The others had called it "the weeping tree," but to her it never wept. It watched. It waited. It remembered. When she was small, she used to lie beneath its branches and trace shapes in the sky with her fingers, pretending they were letters she could never quite read. Her grandmother had once told her that the willow was magic—that it had roots in more than just soil.

She believed her. Even now.

Her bare feet sank slightly into the earth, damp and forgiving. She liked the way the soil held her weight—

quietly, without judgment. The grass cradled her ankles like an old friend. The breeze moved slowly, like breath, like something alive was exhaling.

Daria had not meant to return to this place. It just... pulled her.

Everything in her life lately had felt too loud, too hard, and too uncertain. Decisions stacked like unopened letters. Conversations with too many "should" and not enough space. A sense of not quite belonging that clung to her like static.

However, here, under this tree, the noise dimmed.

She pressed her hand against the bark. It was rough and familiar, and for a moment, she let her eyes close. In the quiet hum between branches, a memory surfaced—her mother's voice, low and tired, brushing her hair behind her ears and saying, "You don't always have to be strong. Just soft enough to stay human."

She had not thought of that in years.

Something inside her shifted. It was not pain exactly. It was a knowing. That something had to change. That the ache she carried was not just hers—it belonged to a version of her that needed to be let go.

She knelt in the grass, tucking her dress beneath her knees, and whispered a single question to the willow.

She did not say it aloud. She did not have to. The willow would know.

The breeze stirred, lifting her hair off her shoulders like the hands of a gentle memory. The light had changed—it slanted through the leaves in ribbons now, warm and golden, like the beginning of something.

And in that moment, still and quiet as the roots beneath her, Daria felt it.

Something was about to begin. Something unseen but already stirring—like the moment before lightning splits the sky, or a dream you almost remember after waking. She did not know what it was yet; only that it would change everything.

Journal Entry 1: For Her Eyes Only

I did not plan to come here. I just ended up beneath the willow tree as it had called me without a sound. Maybe it did. Maybe I just finally heard it again.

It is strange how a place can remember you when you have forgotten yourself. The moment I stepped into its shade, I felt like the girl I used to be. The one who dreamed without permission. The one who made stories out of clouds and whispered promises into tree bark. Where did she go?

Something is shifting in me, and I do not know what it is. It is not sadness. It is not happiness either. That aching in between feeling presses against your ribs like a question with no answer.

I remembered my mother today. Not her face, exactly, but her voice. She said I did not have to be strong all the time. And I believed her back then, but now? I have worn strength like armor for so long; I forgot what it is like to lay it down.

The wind felt different this morning. Not colder. Not warmer. Just… aware. As if it knew I was coming before I did.

I sat under the willow and asked a question I could not say aloud. The tree did not answer, but somehow, I still felt heard.

Tomorrow, I will go back. Not because I must, but because something inside me is tired of hiding.

Chapter 2: A Familiar Song

Daria returned to the willow the next morning, barefoot, but slower this time intentionally. The air was softer than yesterday, as if the wind had been waiting for her, rehearsing its lines overnight.

She had barely slept. Not from worry, but from something else entirely—restlessness disguised as awareness. Her body felt heavy, but her spirit... alert, as if some invisible thread had been pulled loose the day before, and now it was unraveling through her dreams.

This time, she brought something with her: an old leather-bound book, the kind that smelled like memory and dry leaves. The cover was worn smoothly, its corners bent from years of being carried, opened, dropped, and loved. She had not touched it in over a decade. It had sat on her shelf, untouched but not forgotten, waiting for the kind of silence she had finally made space for.

The willow welcomed her without ceremony—no wind gust, no falling leaves, no theatrical rustling. Just presence. Just stillness. She stepped into its shade and let the curtain of green close behind her.

She lowered herself to the ground and sat cross-legged, resting her back against the bark. The coolness of it seeped through her shirt, grounding her as roots might. She let out a breath she had not realized she was holding.

The book stayed closed in her lap.

Her fingers traced the embossed pattern on the cover. They moved slowly, the way they might over a scar. Reverent. Remembering. Then, without fully deciding to, she let it fall open.

The pages had yellowed. The ink had faded. But it was hers. The handwriting in the margins was hers, too—only it did not feel like it belonged to her now. It belonged to a version of her who believed writing things down could keep the world from slipping away.

One note in particular made her pause. Written beside a passage about silence and surrender, she had scribbled, "Remember softness. It is a kind of power."

She exhaled a sound that was not quite a laugh. She did not remember writing that. Yet… it pierced something in her. Not painfully. Not cruelly. Just enough to shake loose whatever she had been bracing against.

For a while, she did not read. She just let the book rest on her knees and watched the sky move slowly through the branches.

Then she heard it.

Not a voice. Not a whisper. A sound—faint and delicate, like a lullaby drifting in from another room. A bird.

The song was simple. Just a few notes. But something about it curled around her ribcage like it knew where her tenderness lived. Like it had been sung before—not yesterday, not last year—but long ago, when her heart was softer and her hands did not always know what to do with stillness.

She closed her eyes.

For a brief second, she imagined the song was not coming from a bird, but from the willow itself. That it had taken her memories and turned them into music. That maybe, just maybe, she was being sung back to herself.

Her mother once told her, "Everything alive speaks. But you have to be quiet long enough to hear what it's saying."

She did not understand it then. She was starting to now.

Opening her eyes, she saw that a single feather had fallen into her lap. Pale gray. Light. Barely there.

Daria smiled—not from joy, but from recognition. She did not know what it meant. But she knew it meant something.

And that was enough.

Journal Entry 2: For Her Eyes Only

This morning felt different. Not in the way big moments feel—but in the way a song lingers even after you stop hearing it.

I brought the old book. The one I used to believe held answers. Now, I am not so sure it ever did. But when I opened it, I saw my own handwriting in the margins. I must have been... what? Seventeen? Nineteen? It said: "Remember softness. It is a kind of power."

I stared at those words as if someone else wrote them— someone I used to be but had not spoken to in years. She sounded wiser than I remembered. Kinder. Less guarded.

I wonder what she would think of me now.

I sat with that book in my lap for a long time. The wind moved slowly, and I tried to match its rhythm. I think I succeeded for a few minutes. I did not feel rushed. I did not feel hollow. I did not feel like I had to fix, prove, or defend anything.

Then... the bird.

Its song was not just sound. It was a memory. It made something behind my ribs soften. I do not know if I cried or if the wind just touched my face in the right way, but for a moment, I felt held. Not by a person. Not even by the willow. But by the fact that I was still here, still capable of hearing beautiful things.

I left with a feather in my hand. I do not know how it got there. I just know I needed it.

Tomorrow, I will return. Not because I am searching, but because I have started to hear the parts of me, I forgot how to listen to.

Chapter 3: The Unnamed Shadow

It was just past twilight when Daria returned to the willow.

The sun had already tucked itself behind the hills, leaving only a bruised edge of gold across the horizon. The air held a different weight now—cooler, heavier, like the evening itself had secrets to carry.

She walked slower than usual. Not because her feet ached, but because something about the moment demanded reverence.

The willow waited in silence.

Its branches dropped lower than before, almost as if the tree itself had grown tired. However, it was not sadness Daria felt as she approached—it was expectation. The kind that lives just before something unspoken happens.

She stepped through the curtain of green and sat cross-legged at the base, pressing her back against the rough bark. The hush wrapped around her, thick and humming. But tonight, something felt... off.

The wind was still. Yet the leaves above her rustled faintly, as if they had secrets that could only be told in a language not meant for ears. She glanced up. No breeze. Yet, the tree moved.

Her hand reached out, steady and slow, pressing gently into the bark. "You know me," she whispered.

The tree gave no reply—but then again, it never needed to.

Then, she felt it.

A shift.

Not outside, but inside her.

It was not fear. It was older than fear. It was the sensation of being seen by something not entirely visible. Something just past the edge of logic. Her skin prickled.

She turned around slowly. Her gaze moved past the roots, toward the edge of the clearing. And there, lying still as bone was a single feather.

Pale. Perfect.

And warm.

Why was it warm?

No bird in sight. No sign of anything that should have left it there. But the way it lay, pointed toward her like an invitation, made her breath hitch.

She rose and walked toward it with deliberate care, kneeling to pick it up. As her fingers touched it, a strange heat radiated through her hand. Not painful. Just alive.

It was waiting for her. She did not know how she knew. She just did.

She held it close to her chest and closed her eyes. A memory—not hers—fluttered through her mind: a quiet sob behind a

closed door. The smell of earth. A voice saying, "Don't forget who you were before they told you who to be."

Her heart ached as if it were remembering something it had not been told yet.

That is when she heard it: a whisper with no source. Not words. Not sound. Just presence.

Something was there. Something ancient. Not threatening. Not warm. Just… watching.

The willow creaked softly behind her.

She did not run. She did not speak. She just stood with the feather clutched in her hand, the sky darkening above her, the ground holding her weight without question.

Journal Entry 3: For Her Eyes Only

Tonight felt different. The silence was heavier. The willow did not just stand still—it waited. And so did I.

There is something here I cannot name yet. A shadow, maybe. But not the kind you run from—the kind you turn toward because you know… somehow… it already knows you.

The feather was warm when I touched it. How is that possible? No sun. No life around. No reason. Just warmth. As if it had been held by something not made of hands. It did not scare me, but it also did not comfort me. It just made me aware. As I was not alone in the way, I thought I was.

Then there was the whisper. I could not make out the words—if there even were any. But it moved through me as if memory does. Like something trying to return.

What if it is not the world that is changing?

What if it is just me, finally shedding the noise, the shape I molded myself into, just to survive?

There is a voice in me that I have forgotten how to listen to. But I think it is starting to speak again.

I will go back tomorrow. Not to chase answers— but to honor the question that has finally begun to bloom.

Chapter 4: The Dream Beneath the Leaves

That night, Daria dreamt of feathers.

They did not fall, they floated, suspended in the kind of stillness that feels louder than noise. The sky was not sky. Deep indigo laced stitched fabric— with threads of silver, as if someone had embroidered constellations just for her.

She was not walking. She was drifting. Not on wings, but on memory.

There was no ground beneath her feet. There was no wind, but her hair moved like it was underwater.

She was not afraid.

The willow appeared ahead, not as she knew it, but magnified, its roots curling downward like tendrils of a great truth. Its bark glowed faintly, as though stories were etched beneath the surface, illuminated only by dream light.

She reached toward one of the branches, and it lowered to meet her hand. The moment they touched, light bloomed. Shapes rose from the shadows—half-people, half-selves. They shimmered with the translucence of memory.

One turned to face her.

She gasped.

It had her eyes.

But younger.

Wilder.

Unbroken.

She opened her mouth to speak, but the version of her did not need words. She simply reached out and placed a hand on Daria's chest.

Daria flinched. And woke.

The room was dark. Her pillow was damp. Her fingers were curled tightly around her bed sheet like it was the last piece of certainty in the world.

On the nightstand, the feather from the clearing. Still pale. Still warm.

She stared at it.

For a moment, she did not breathe. Then she whispered into the dark:

"I want to remember."

Not just the dream.

But the parts of herself she had exiled. The girl who sang before she learned shame. The softness she was told to fear. The wildness she buried under politeness and duty.

In the morning, she did not go straight to the willow.

She walked first to the stream.

The water was low, whispering over the rocks, telling secrets that could only be said in silence. Daria sat on a smooth stone and dipped her feet in. The cold bit her toes, but she did not pull back.

The memory of the dream still curled in her belly like firelight. Not burning. Warming.

She looked up to the trees and thought: What if that girl—my girl—was always watching? What if every time I whispered doubt, she heard? What if she never stopped believing in me?

The thought made her heart ache.

She whispered to the wind, "I'm trying."

And the wind, as if to reply, rustled the leaves once—no more.

When she returned to the willow, it looked different. Taller somehow. Quieter. More real.

She sat beneath it, this time not seeking guidance, but offering something. Her breath. Her presence. Her unspoken promise:

I will not forget her again.

Journal Entry 4: For Her Eyes Only

Last night… was not a dream.

Not in the usual way. It felt like a memory. But not mine—not fully. More like… borrowed memory. Shared soul-space. A place I forgot existed inside me.

There were feathers. Floating, endless. No weight. No gravity. Like truth unanchored.

Then I saw her. The girl I used to be. Before the layers. Before the rules. Before I learned how to silence myself politely.

She did not speak. She did not need to. She just was—wild, luminous, and staring at me as if I were the one who had disappeared.

When I woke up, I felt like I had been dropped from a great height. My body was heavy, but something in me had unlatched. As if a window opened in a room, I did not know I had locked.

I did not run to the willow today. I needed space. Time. Therefore, I went to the stream and let the water talk. It whispered that I am still in there. That softness does not vanish. It just waits.

I think she has been waiting for me to remember.

And I do now. Not everything. But enough to say this:

I will not forget her again.

Chapter 5: The First Word

There had always been silence between the roots of the willow. But today, something broke.

Daria did not arrive with an offering. She did not come wrapped in ritual. She came with a single, trembling word— one she had not dared to say in years.

It was not a name. It was not a plea. It was a whisper: "Me."

The sound felt unfamiliar in her mouth. Too soft. Too powerful. Like setting fire to a feather.

She stepped forward until her toes touched the roots. Her hands did not shake this time, but her voice did.

"I've forgotten how to belong to myself."

She did not expect the willow to respond. But something in the earth vibrated—low and steady, like acknowledgment.

She sat slowly, drawing her knees to her chest, staring down at her fingers. They looked like her mother's now. Tired. Capable. I'm still searching for softness.

The breeze passed through her hair, catching her off guard with its gentleness. As it knew how long she had been bracing for harshness instead.

She closed her eyes and whispered again:

"Me."

As if saying it enough might finally make it safe.

Earlier that morning, she opened a drawer she had not touched in months. Inside: a folded letter, yellowing at the edges, sealed but never sent.

The handwriting was hers—messy and sharp, like someone trying to write faster than her heart could speak.

She had not remembered writing it. However, the moment she touched it, something inside her began to weep.

She brought it with her.

Now, under the willow, she unfolded the letter with careful fingers. The ink had blurred at the signature, as if tears had tried to edit her name.

It read:

"To the part of me that gave everything and still felt empty—

I am sorry no one taught you boundaries before you broke. I am sorry you thought silence was safer than honesty. I am sorry they called you 'too much' when you were just enough for your own story.

You are not a wound. You are not a warning. You are a woman who lived through fire and still smells like flowers.

Come home. I'll meet you there."

She folded it again, pressed it to her chest, and for the first time, she did not cry.

The clearing did not shift.

The birds did not sing loudly.

However, Daria felt different. Not bigger. Not bolder. Just truer.

And that was enough.

When she finally stood, she placed the letter beneath a stone at the tree's base. Not hidden. Just resting. Like something that had earned its place in the soil.

Then she looked up.

Not in the sky. But at herself, reflected in the breeze, echoed in the bark, present in the breath she just took without permission.

"I said my first word today," she whispered, smiling. "And it was me."

Journal Entry 5: For Her Eyes Only

Today I said my name.

Not out loud. Not fully. But I whispered it into the roots of that tree like it was a spell.

"Me."

It sounds small written here. But it felt enormous in my throat. Like lifting something ancient off my chest. Like unlocking a door, I did not even know I had sealed shut.

I think I have spent so many years being a version of myself that was easy to love—quiet enough, useful enough, unbothered enough—that I forgot what it was like to exist without performing.

I want to remember the version of me who danced when no one watched. Who cried without shame? Who believed being soft did not make her weak—it made her real.

I found an old letter I had written to myself. I do not remember when. But it knew me. Knew how tired I was. How badly I wanted someone, anyone, to tell me I did not have to hold everything together all the time.

I think I wrote it in the middle of breaking. And I think I left it behind because I was not ready to hear the truth.

However, I am ready now.

Therefore, this is my truth tonight: I am not starting over.
I am starting honestly. And maybe that's better.

Chapter 6: Echoes of Lavender

The candle had burned down to its final breath by morning. Its wax had pooled like a quiet surrender beneath the roots of the willow.

Daria arrived early, even before the dew had finished walking. The sky, still drowsy, spilled light in watercolor shades—peach, lilac, and rose. The grass was cool and forgiving, brushing against her ankles like it remembered her from some softer time.

She stood still for a long moment before entering the clearing.

Something had changed.

The air carried a whisper of lavender. Not the scent of a flower still in bloom, but the memory of one—the kind that clings to old linens and echoing rooms. Daria froze mid-step, breath caught between memory and dream.

Lavender.

Her mother's hands used to smell like that. Lavender oil and clean sheets, and whispered lullabies. Daria had not thought of that for years.

It came back all at once—a pillowcase tucked gently beneath her cheek, a soft hum, a woman's voice saying, "Let the dreams be kind tonight, my little feather."

She blinked hard. The memory brushed past her like a breeze.

She knelt near the willow, noticing the wax from the night before. It had hardened into a silken puddle around the base of the tree, like a forgotten offering. She reached out, touched it gently.

Warm.

Still warm.

Why?

She sat cross-legged and let the moment anchor her. This was not a ceremony. This was presence. Something deeper than ritual—something sacred in its simplicity.

She found a flat stone nearby and carefully loosened the wax from the bark. Then she reached into her pocket, pulled out a linen square she did not even remember packing, and wrapped the wax inside.

Without knowing why, she whispered, "For later."

She touched the feather hanging from her neck. Her fingers trembled—not from fear, but reverence.

The feather had changed her.

Not because it held magic.

Because it held memory.

Later that day, she sat at her desk—bare wood, no adornments—and opened a blank page.

At the top, she wrote: "What I remember when I forget myself."

The first line was shaky. The second felt truer. The third surprised her. Memories poured out like breath she did not know she had been holding. Lavender. Laughter. The way her mother danced while folding laundry. The warmth of hands that braided her hair. The grief of forgetting how it felt to be cared for.

The page filled slowly. Line by line. Life by life.

She returned to the clearing that evening. Not to bring anything. Not to bury. Not to search.

Just to be.

The willow stood quiet. However, its branches swayed just once, just enough to let her know you are not alone.

And for the first time, that was enough.

Journal Entry 6: For Her Eyes Only

Lavender.

Isn't it wild how one smell can unlock a thousand unopened boxes inside you?

I did not expect to remember her hands today. I did not expect to cry.

But there it was—in the air, in the grass, in the way the light touched the leaves: a memory so soft it hurt. My mother's voice. My name is wrapped in tenderness. That one lullaby she never finished singing.

There are moments when the past does not knock. It arrives. And you just have to make space for it, no matter how tightly you have locked the door.

I carried home a piece of wax from the willow tree. It is nothing. It is everything.

It felt warm when I touched it, and I do not know why. However, I wrapped it like it mattered. Because it did.

Because I am learning that care does not need logic. It just needs presence.

Later, I wrote for the first time without forcing it. No purpose. No audience. Just breathe on a page.

And it felt like healing.

Not the loud kind. The kind that does not need applause.

I am not ready to forgive the world yet. But maybe I am ready to forgive myself for forgetting who I was before it got loud.

Lavender made me remember. And for now, that's enough.

Chapter 7: The Release

The sky was silver with clouds when Daria returned to the willow.

Not stormy. Not clear. Just… suspended. Like the day itself, I did not know what it wanted to be. She walked slowly, her breath tighter than usual, her chest full of something she could not name—but felt.

She did not bring a candle or a book. Just herself. Just the ache in her chest that had grown louder over the past few days.

The grass was damp, and the wind was unusually warm for the season. The tree swayed—not lazily, but with intention, as if it were trying to shake something loose.

Her fingers gripped the soil beneath her.

And without warning—no build-up, no soft beginning— she broke.

The wind stirred more forcefully than usual. The willow did not just sway—it shivered. The branches trembled, as they were carrying stories too old for language.

Daria dropped to her knees before the tree. No ceremony. No grace. Just collapse. Her legs did not ask for permission.

Her heart did not wait for the right moment. It came—like water bursting from a crack.

She did not cry. She sobbed.

The sobbing came fast and full, pulled from somewhere she did not know still existed. It was not graceful. It was not poetic. It was primal.

Messy. Loud. Undeniable.

"I miss her," she whispered into her hands. "I miss the way she smelled like tea and safety. I miss the way she used to call me feather—like I was something light instead of something heavy."

She pressed her hand to her chest as if she were trying to keep her heart inside.

"I don't want to be afraid anymore. I don't want to pretend I'm not shattered in places I can't name."

Tears soaked the cuffs of her sleeves. Her body folded in on itself.

The willow bent just slightly, as if listening more closely.

Or maybe it did not.

But in that moment, Daria believed it had.

She stayed curled up for what felt like hours.

She did not apologize to the tree. She did not try to pull herself together. She simply was—a vessel of grief and longing, cracking in the safety of roots and earth.

Letting the silence sponge her tears. Letting the dirt hold the weight of grief she had never shared.

Then...

Something shifted.

Not outside.

Inside.

She sat up slowly and reached into her coat pocket.

Not a feather. Not a letter. But a lavender sachet—hand-tied from her mother's old tin of dried petals.

She pressed it to her lips, breathing in everything she had lost and everything she still carried.

Then she dug gently into the earth at the base of the tree.

She did not bury it.

She planted it.

"I'm ready," she whispered.

Not a hope. Not a plea. A declaration.

When she stood, she felt... different.

Not whole. But it cleared up. Like space had finally been made inside her.

As she walked away from the tree, the wind circled her, not cold, not pushing, just wrapping.

Like it had witnessed everything.

And it approved.

Journal Entry 7: For Her Eyes Only

Today I fell apart.

Not gently. Not quietly. It was not poetic. It was ugly. Loud. Snot and saltwater and the kind of sobbing that echoes in your bones long after the air goes still.

I did not plan it. I did not let go like some brave metaphor. I exploded—like a dam that could not hold anymore.

I said her name aloud today. My mother. The one whose absence carved rooms inside me that I keep trying to decorate with strength.

I miss her. I miss me, the version of me she left behind, who still believed in being held.

I pressed that lavender sachet into the earth as if it were my chest. I whispered, "Take it. Grow something from it." And the dirt… it felt warm. It felt ready.

Like maybe, the earth understands grief better than we do.

I think breaking is sacred. Nobody tells you that. They tell you to breathe, to journal, to walk it off. But sometimes healing is collapsing in the exact place that broke you and daring to rebuild anyway.

I do not know who I am after this cry. However, I feel more real than who I was before.

And that… that is something.

Chapter 8: Where Silence Blooms

The day after the storm of her own unspoken tears, Daria did not go searching for revelation. She simply walked. No candle. No intention. No plan.

The path to the willow was familiar now, like a foot-worn trail back to a version of herself, she was learning to trust again.

Yet… something had changed.

The clearing was bathed in soft morning light, the kind that made shadows feel tender. The willow stood still, but not silent. It breathed through leaves, through breeze, through the very soil it rooted in.

Daria felt it before she saw it. That sense of being seen.

At the base of the willow, something green had emerged. Tiny shoots. Fragile, trembling leaves curling up from the earth. She blinked, recognizing the spot.

Right where she had buried the lavender.

She knelt beside them. Reached out with hesitant fingers. Brushed the leaves as if they were newborn things, and whispered:

"Hello."

It was not a habit. It was not hope. It was recognition.

She did not cry. She did not ache. She simply was.

The air around her hummed. Not like a sound, but like permission.

Yet she did something she had not done in years.

She lay down in the grass.

Arms wide. Eyes closed. The soul opens.

The sun touched her face like a blessing. A bird chirped once, and the wind sighed as if it knew her secret and kept it anyway.

Her breath slowed. Her thoughts softened.

And she realized: this was what she had been chasing in all those rituals, in all that searching, in all the ways she had tried to earn peace.

Stillness.

Not numbness. Not the frozen kind of silence that fear demands. But the alive kind. The kind that listens. That holds.

In addition, suddenly, Daria was not waiting anymore.

She was being.

Later, she stood, only a few steps beyond the tree. Just enough to see what lay beyond the curve of the clearing. There was more forest. More unknown.

She did not go into it.

Not yet.

But she had moved.

And that shift—small, silent, sacred—was enough.

Journal Entry 8: For Her Eyes Only

Today I felt like breathing for the first time after holding it in for years.

Not a dramatic breath. A quiet one. The kind that finds you when you are not searching. The kind you almost forgot how to take.

I did not carry anything with me to the clearing today. No flame. No notebook. No questions. Just myself.

Moreover, for once, that was enough.

I saw new shoots sprouting where I left the lavender sachet. Green, trembling, impossibly brave. Like the earth had heard me whisper, and whispered back: "You are growing, too."

I touched the leaves. They were soft like skin, like memory. It was like reaching into something buried in me and finding it still alive.

I did not cry. I did not ache. I did not spiral into thought. I just lay back in the grass, arms wide, and let the sky press its blue into my bones.

I listened to everything. To the breeze nudging the leaves. To a bird I could not name. To the way, silence no longer felt empty—but completely, completely.

Maybe healing is not about getting louder. Maybe it is about being still enough to hear yourself again.

I did not go far today.

But I moved.

And that movement—it felt like forgiveness.

Chapter 9: The Stranger with Quiet Eyes

Daria was walking further now.

Not far—never too far—but enough to feel the stretch. The whisper of "what else is out there?" had turned into a gentle pull, not of urgency, but of invitation.

On this afternoon, she followed a path that curved just beyond the willow's view. It went through ferns and tall grass, kissed by dandelion seeds drifting like snow.

That is when she saw him.

A figure, seated on a fallen log near the bend of a stream. He was not imposing. In fact, he looked like he belonged to the woods, as if he had grown from the earth and simply chosen to sit still that day. His coat was worn, his hands relaxed, and his gaze was fixed on the water.

He did not hear her approach at first. She paused a few steps back, unsure whether to move forward or leave the moment undisturbed.

There was something sacred about the way he watched the stream. Like he was listening. Like he understood the language of moving water.

She stayed there in silence, studying him—not with judgment, but with curiosity.

There was something familiar in his stillness. Something that made her ache and soften at the same time.

He looked like someone who had once been broken but had chosen not to close.

Then, as if sensing her thoughts, he turned.

His eyes were not startled. They were not guarded either. They were... open. Quiet. Deep. The color of dusk after a long day.

For a moment, neither of them spoke. Somehow, the silence felt full. Like a page between two letters.

She took another step and sat on a nearby stone, careful not to disturb the hush between them.

Then, after a long pause, he said without turning:

"This place heals."

His voice was soft, unpolished. Like a note played on an old violin.

Daria nodded. "Yes," she whispered. "It does."

They sat like that. Two strangers. Not looking for answers. Not seeking comfort. Just sharing space.

She did not ask his name. And he did not ask her.

On the other hand, in the way the light fell between them, in the way the stream curved at their feet, something unspoken passed.

Not a spark. But a knowing.

She did not feel lonely. And that... felt new.

After some time, she stood.

He looked up again, but did not stop her.

As she turned to go, he spoke once more. Just four words.

"Maybe I'll see you."

She smiled—small, real—and whispered back:

"Maybe you already have."

And she walked home differently.

Not faster. Not slower. Just... with something beside her she had not carried before.

Journal Entry 9: For Her Eyes Only

Today I met someone. However, I do not know his name. And maybe that is the most beautiful part.

I saw him by the stream, like a dream with calloused hands. He looked like someone who understood loss. Not because he was broken, but because he did not run from the breaking.

He did not fill the space with words. He did not try to teach, reach, or explain. He just… was.

And in that was-ness, I felt seen.

I did not ask who he was. Because some souls do not need introductions. They echo into you.

He said, "This place heals."

Not like a line from a poem. More like he bled those words into the ground before saying them.

We did not touch. However, something touched me.

And when I left, he said, "Maybe I'll see you."

Here is the truth, though: He already did.

Not like the others do. Not through the performance, I have learned to wear.

He saw the quiet. The ache. The girl who is not always brave. The woman who is tired of pretending.

Moreover, it made me wonder—how many people we have missed, simply because we did not know how to sit with their silence?

Maybe this was not a meeting. Maybe it was a memory.

Yet maybe I will return tomorrow… not to find him again, but to find that version of myself he awakened, or… to learn more about.

Chapter 10: The Echo of His Voice- The Father

The stranger's voice still lingered in Daria's mind long after he disappeared into the mist. It was not just the words he had spoken; it was something deeper, something achingly familiar—like a thread she had once clutched tightly and then, over the years, let slip through her fingers.

Daria sat by the river's edge, hugging her knees to her chest. The sun was low, laying golden fingers across the water. The breeze stirred the tall grasses, carrying with it the scent of damp earth and memory.

Closing her eyes, she leaned into the hush of the moment. It was there, in the tender silence, that another voice rose—a voice she had not heard in so many seasons she had almost convinced herself it had been imagined.

Her father's voice.

"When the world pushes you away, little bird," he had said, once upon a time, crouching beside her after she had fallen from a tree, "you must plant your feet even deeper into the ground. Let the storm come. Let it roar. You stay rooted."

She had been a child then, fierce and impatient, chasing after wildflowers and cloud dreams. At the time, she had barely listened; too busy trying to wipe the dirt from her scraped palms, too eager to prove that she was already strong.

"Be strong," he had told her, his hand warm and steady on her back, "but never lose your softness. That's where your real strength lives."

She hadn't understood. Not truly. Not until life had broken her open again and again, scattering pieces she no longer knew how to gather.

The river's song grew louder in her ears, as if the water itself carried the memories forward.

She remembered another time: a bitter winter afternoon when she had come home from school with fists clenched and cheeks burning. Someone had laughed at her—called her too quiet, too strange, too soft. She had stormed into the house, vowing never to trust anyone again.

Her father had sat her down by the fire, his face lit by the glow of the flames. He had not dismissed her anger. He had not told her to harden or to strike back. Instead, he had wrapped a heavy blanket around her shoulders and simply said,

"You are not meant to be like them, Daria. The world needs your tenderness more than it knows. Even when it doesn't deserve it."

At the time, she had thought he was wrong. She had vowed to become sharper, louder, and colder. Moreover, for a long time, she had succeeded. She had worn her resilience like armor, wielding it like a weapon against disappointment.

But where had it led her? Here. Alone beside a river, aching for a voice she had once dismissed.

The stranger's presence had unsettled her not because he was foreign, but because he mirrored something lost within her—a softness that could weather storms without becoming stone.

Daria opened her eyes to the twilight spreading across the sky. The first stars were waking, their pale light blinking uncertainly against the darkening blue.

She spoke aloud without meaning to, her voice hoarse from disuse:

"I'm sorry I didn't listen."

The river carried her words away, but she knew— somewhere beyond sight—he heard her.

A memory floated forward, vivid and tender:

One evening, when the world felt too big and her dreams too small, she had crawled into her father's lap, ashamed of her fears.

"What if I'm not strong enough?" she had whispered.

He had chuckled, the sound low and warm.

"Then you will grow stronger. Not by fighting harder, but by staying true to your heart."

He had pressed her palm against his chest.

"This is where the greatest strength lives. Not in fists. Not in shouting. Here."

And now, years later, Daria pressed her hand against her chest, feeling the fragile, stubborn thrum of her heart. It was still beating. Still believing. Still hers.

Tears slid down her cheeks, not heavy, anguished sobs, but quiet, grateful tears. She had survived. Not because she had become hard. But because, despite everything, she had never fully let go of who she was. She had bent but not broken. She had cracked but not crumbled.

She let the river cradle her grief and her gratitude alike, letting them flow together into something new.

Then, as the stars multiplied overhead, something extraordinary happened. She heard him—not in the air, not with her ears, but deep inside the place where memory and soul intertwine.

"I am so proud of you, little bird."

The words rose from within her, from the marrow of her being, as if he had planted them there long ago, waiting for this very moment to bloom.

A soft gasp escaped her lips. She smiled through the blur of tears, the kind of smile that hurts and heals all at once.

"I missed you," she whispered.

"I know," came the reply, not in sound, but in certainty. A gentle wind brushed her hair back from her face, almost like a caress. Daria, for the first time in a long while, did not feel alone.

The stranger, the river, the voice of her father—they had

all conspired to remind her: She was not lost. She was not broken. She was becoming.
Feather by feather.
Memory by memory.
Breath by breath.

She looked at her reflection in the water, and this time, she did not search for flaws or fractures. She saw a woman made of stories, stitched together by love and longing and quiet, stubborn hope.

And standing behind her, just for a moment before dissolving into the ripples, was the outline of a man with kind eyes and a patient smile.

Not a ghost. Not a shadow. But a blessing.

"Whenever you doubt, listen for my voice," he had once told her. "It will always lead you back to yourself."

Daria rose to her feet, her body aching from sitting so long, but her spirit lighter. She placed her hand over her heart, sealing the promise there.

The world might still try to bend her. Life might still be unfair, but she would meet it with open hands and a steady soul.

She would remember.

And she would walk forward—not as someone armored against the world, but as someone rooted, softened, and stronger than she had ever known.

Journal entry 10: For her eyes only

Tonight, by the river, I met him again.
Not in the flesh, but in the folds of memory, in the quiet
that lives between heartbeats.

I thought I had lost him.
I thought the world had hardened me too much to ever
find my way back to his voice.
But he was there.
He had been there all along.

I realize now that strength was never about shutting out
the world or hiding my tenderness behind walls.
It was about planting my roots deeper when storms
came.
It was about bending, not breaking.
It was about choosing love, even when fear was easier.

Father, if you can hear me —
I am listening now.
Truly listening.

Your voice echoes inside me like a quiet song:
Stay rooted, little bird. Stay soft. That is your true
strength.

Tonight, I made a promise to myself:

I will walk forward with open hands.
I will meet the world not as a warrior in battle, but as a
tree standing firm, offering shade, offering beauty,
offering truth.

And when doubt creeps in — as it will —
I will place my hand over my heart, where your lessons
still live, and I will listen.
I will remember who I am becoming.
Feather by feather.
Memory by memory.
Breath by breath.

You did not lose me.
I am finding my way home.
And I am carrying your voice with me, always.
– Daria

Chapter 11: The Voice Beneath the Willow

Daria returned to the willow with something new inside her.

Not just peace. Not just memory.

Nevertheless, a voice.

For the first time since she could remember, she did not arrive to listen. She came to speak.

She walked barefoot, not because it felt poetic, but because she wanted the earth to know her. To hold her weight like it had all along.

The feather around her neck glinted faintly in the morning light. The tree's shadow reached for her like an old friend, not in welcome, but in witness.

She did not sit. She stood.

"I've been quiet for so long," she said aloud, her voice unfamiliar but strong. "I thought healing meant disappearing. Shrinking. Whispering into silence."

A breeze stirred the leaves like soft applause.

"But it's not," she continued. "Healing is remembering how to take up space."

Her hand rose to the bark—her palm pressing into the grooves she had traced a hundred times. This time, she was not seeking comfort.

She was giving thanks.

"You heard me," she whispered. "Even when I could not hear myself."

The night before, she had written something. Not in her journal. On real paper. Torn from the edge of an old notebook. No fancy ink. No polished prose.

Just the truth.

A letter.

To no one.

To herself.

I forgive you. You survived. Now, go live.

She folded it once. Then again. Pressed it flat beneath her palm. Now, beneath the willow, she tucked it into a hollow where the roots curled like fingers.

Not hidden. Not buried. Just… placed.

She exhaled. A long, trembling breath. Not because she was afraid. Because she was not.

The clearing was still quiet. However, it was not empty.

It felt full of breath, of light, of truth.

Then she turned.

To leave?

Not quite.

TO BEGIN!

At the edge of the clearing, she paused and looked back one final time.

"Thank you," she said softly.

Not to the tree. Not to the sky.

To the girl she had once been. To the woman she was becoming.

Then—barefoot, shoulders back, hair loose in the wind—she walked away.

Not as someone who was healing.

But as someone whole.

THE BEGINNING (she whispered).

Journal Entry 11: For Her Eyes Only

I spoke today.

Not in whispers. Not in scribbles. Not in metaphors, so I would not be scared myself.

Out loud. As I believed, I deserved to hear my voice again.

The willow did not reply. However, it did not need to. Because today, for the first time, I did.

I stood there, not like someone hoping to be understood. But as someone ready to understand herself.

I said words I have been trying to write for years.

I FORGIVE YOU. YOUT SURVIVED. NOW GO LIVE!

I left those words tucked into the roots. Where they could root into the earth and maybe bloom into something I will never see—but someone else will feel.

I am not just healing anymore. I am becoming.

The girl who walks into a room as if she belongs there.

The woman who no longer folds herself to make others more comfortable.

The soul that knows softness is not a flaw—it is a gift.

The willow was not the destination. It was the mirror.

But now?

I AM THE STORY.

And I am just getting started.

Chapter 12: The Return of the Raven

The morning was golden, the kind of golden that feels earned. The kind that glows like a secret kept safe through the night.

Daria walked slowly, her fingertips brushing the tops of tall grass as she blessed the earth with her presence. The silence was thick but not heavy. It was the kind of silence that meant something was about to happen.

Then she saw it.

A single black feather. Not drifting. Not lying. Planted.

Right in the middle of the path.

Not soft like the one she wore around her neck—this one was heavier. Sleek. Purposeful. RAVEN.

Her heart jumped.

Ravens meant something. They always had. When she was a child, she believed they brought omens. Bad luck. Death. As only her grandmother used to say, "Ravens don't bring endings—they bring messages. You're just not always ready to hear them."

Now, standing in front of this feather, her breath caught in her chest. She did not want to pick it up, but she did. Of course she did.

It was warm.

Again.

The air changed.

A single cry rang out above her—low, thick, guttural. She did not look up right away.

However, she knew.

When she finally lifted her gaze, there it was perched high in the willow, black feathers gleaming like obsidians in the morning light.

The raven tilted its head once, twice—as if sizing her up. Then it blinked.

And Daria remembered.

She had seen one before. The day everything fell apart.

She had not understood its call then. She thought it was just noise, or maybe it had been trying to say something.

She watched as if it took a small hop down the branch. Then another. Closer.

Then, it dropped another feather.

Not carelessly. Not by accident. Given.

Daria stepped forward and caught it midair, and in her chest, something ancient whispered: *You are ready to be seen.*

She stood taller. The wind lifted her hair as if it had something to say.

The raven let out one last cry, then soared upward, cutting through the clouds like a blade made of myth.

Daria did not cry. She did not smile.

She just stood there, hand open, feathers in her palm, and let the know settle.

Later that evening, she returned to the willow with both feathers. She sat at the base and braided the raven feather into her necklace, right beside the soft one. Black and white. Shadow and light.

"I'm not hiding anymore," she whispered.

No ceremony. No vows. Just a truth spoken into the roots.

She stayed long after the sun had dropped below the trees, until even the sky turned quiet.

And when she rose, it was not the girl who left.

It was the woman the world had been waiting for.

Journal Entry 12: For Her Eyes Only

A raven came today.

And no, it was not dramatic. It did not sound like thunder. It did not fly in circles like some mythic omen.

It just… landed. And watched.

I saw it before I heard it. A black feather on the path, bold as ink on a white page. I did not pick it up right away. I just stared as if it might evaporate if I got too close.

Ravens used to scare me. Not because of what they are. But because of what I thought they meant, endings. Warnings. Loss.

The last time I saw one, my life cracked down the middle. No one knew that. No one could know that.

I had stuffed that memory so deep, it was practically fossilized.

But today, the raven did not bring fear. It brought... an invitation.

It dropped another feather. Deliberate. A gesture. A sign. A question I had not asked. On the other hand, maybe one I was too afraid to speak aloud:

Am I ready to be seen?

I did not say yes. Nevertheless, I did not look away either.

That counts for something.

Because that is where the real beginning lives—not in grand confessions, but in the quiet refusal to disappear.

I picked up the feather. My hands shook. It was warm. Again. Why are they always warm?

No fire nearby. No sunbeam caught on it. Just... warmth. As if it came from a place where things matter more than logic.

I tucked it next to the other one in my journal ribbon— light and dark, soft and sharp, one for memory, one for presence.

Then I just stood there. Under the gaze of a bird that felt older than time and twice as honest.

It did not blink. Did not move. Just saw me.

And I let it.

There is something different about today. As if I stepped into a version of myself, I forgot it was possible.

Not louder. Not braver. Just... unhidden.

I do not know where this is going, but I know now that I am not walking alone.

Because something ancient met my gaze and did not flinch.

What if I can do that too, like the raven?

Then maybe I am already flying.

Chapter 13: The Village Beneath the Willow

The roots of the willow had always called to her—silent, deep, pulsing with a kind of ancient stillness.

That day, Daria stood before them longer than usual. The feathers braided into her hair stirred in the breeze, but her body was still.

There was a hollow, just large enough for her to press her hand into. She had touched it before, but today felt different. The bark was warmer than it should have been, as if it held a breath waiting to exhale.

She leaned forward. Pressed her palm. Closed her eyes.

And fell forward.

Not physically. Not quite, but the moment she let go, the world shifted.

The smell of earth thickened. The sound of birds vanished. The light... changed.

She opened her eyes and blinked into the quiet.

She was standing in a village.

But it was not the one she knew. This one breathed differently.

The homes were shaped from clay and wood, curved like a song. Smoke curled from chimneys into lavender skies.

Children darted between trees that whispered in a language she almost recognized. Women knelt beside streams, humming lullabies that made her chest ache with nostalgia.

Everything was soft. Everything was old, and everything felt like her.

As she walked, no one stared. Yet everyone saw her.

A boy nodded. A woman smiled. An elder bowed ever so slightly as she passed.

She did not speak. She did not need to. The place spoke through feeling. Through memory.

The path led her to a round, open space in the center of the village. Moreover, there, beneath a smaller willow, sat a girl.

Small. Barefoot. Hair tangled and eyes wide.

She looked up.

Daria gasped.

It was her.

Not a twin. Not a trick. Just herself, younger—maybe ten, maybe eleven. The girl with a voice too loud for some, a heart too tender for the world, and a silence planted deep by fear.

The girl blinked once, and then asked softly:

"Why did you leave me?"

Daria fell to her knees. "I didn't mean to," she whispered. "I thought I had to forget you in order to survive."

The girl tilted her head. "But you promised we'd stay together."

Tears spilled before she could answer.

"I know," Daria breathed. "I know. I'm sorry."

The girl studied her, then stood and stepped forward. She touched Daria's chest.

"Are you still in there?"

Daria nodded.

"Then come home."

When Daria opened her eyes, she was back.

The willow above her.

The feather on her chest.

However, the girl? She was still with her—inside her now. Not waiting. Not abandoned. Reunited.

The roots hummed.

Daria exhaled.

And whispered, "I remember."

Journal Entry 13: For Her Eyes Only

Today, I stepped into a village that should not exist.

Yet—it knew me. It held me like a breath held too long. It looked at me with the quiet gaze of a place that had been waiting patiently for my return.

I did not walk in with courage. I walked in with curiosity. I did not arrive as a hero. I arrived as someone was unfinished.

However, the village did not ask for polish. It asked for a presence, and I gave it all I had.

There was a smaller willow at the center. Moreover, beneath it, her.

The girl I used to be. Shoeless, messy-haired, blinking at me like I was the one who had gone missing.

When she asked me why I left... I could barely answer.

How do you explain that sometimes, in order to survive, you have to abandon the parts of yourself that dream too loudly?

How do you say, "I missed you" and "I did not know how to carry you" in the same breath?

She did not cry. She did not rage. She just listened.

And I felt my spine crack open from the weight of that mercy.

I realized something today: We do not grow out of our inner child. We bury her beneath adult armor and pretend she never asked for anything.

Nevertheless, she waits. Every time we lie and say, "I'm fine." Every time we say yes when we mean no. Every time we apologize for needing softness.

She waits.

And today, I knelt at her feet. Not to beg for forgiveness, but to make space.

For her. For me. For us.

I walked through the village as dusk painted the sky lavender. Every face nodded without a word.

I felt known. Not by name, only by truth.

One woman brushed my shoulder with her shawl, and something passed through me like a lullaby. A boy with ink-stained fingers pointed to the willow like it was a beacon. And the stream at the village's edge? It hummed in a language I did not speak but understood.

There's magic in the places we forget to believe in.

There is healing in letting memory walk beside you, instead of behind you.

If anyone ever reads this:

There is a version of you that still believes in wonder. There is a version of you that still believes in you.

Do not wait until you are whole. Go now. Find her. Sit beside her. Let her speak and listen as if it were the first language you ever learned.

Because somewhere in the village beneath your bones, she is waiting by the willow.

She has been calling you home the whole time.

Chapter 14: The First Time I Spoke

The next morning, Daria returned to the willow with a quiet ache in her chest. Not sorrow—readiness.

The wind was gentle. The air smelled like rain that had not yet arrived. She stepped to the roots again, her hand knowing exactly where to rest.

She whispered nothing. She just trusted.

Like the day before, the world began to shift.

Earth thickened. Sky bent. Memory breathed.

When she opened her eyes, she was in the village once more.

Only this time, she was not alone.

The clearing in the center had gathered faces—villagers from every corner. They stood around the willow that marked the heart of this place. Some held small bundles. Others simply stood with open hands.

Daria took a step forward. They made space for her.

In the corner of the crowd, half-hidden in shadow but fully present, was the girl.

Little Daria. Sitting cross-legged. Silent. Watching.

Her presence was a tether. A promise. You are not doing this without me.

Daria stepped into the circle. Daria looked at her, scared, not knowing if people would judge or listen. The moment of truth came, and the little girl was there.

She looked at them, not as a teacher, not as a prophet. Just… as someone who remembered. Still, though, she was ready to run again, only this time, the girl was looking at her.

"I used to think I was the only one," she said softly.

A shift in the crowd. No one moved, but everyone leaned in.

"I thought silence kept me safe. That if I never said the truth out loud, it couldn't hurt me."

She looked down at her hands. "But it did hurt. It hollowed me."

"I carried that hollow into every room, every relationship, and every version of myself."

She raised her eyes. "I was not weak. I was scared. And I was still worthy of love."

I used to think love was a prize you had to earn.
That it came wrapped in conditions, hidden behind walls I

could never climb high enough to reach.
To me, love was something you begged for in silence.
Something you tried to deserve by being quieter, better,
less of a burden.
It was a door always half-closed, a hand almost reaching
for mine but pulling back before our fingers could touch.

I learned to see love as something fragile, something that
could shatter the moment I asked for too much or showed
too little strength.

I thought if I broke, even a little, no one would stay.
No one would want the cracked pieces.
So I built masks instead of bridges.

I hid every trembling part of me behind smiles too tight,
apologies too quick.
I called it strength.
But it was fear.
It was loneliness wearing armor.

Deep down, I still craved it.
Not the kind of love that demanded perfection.
Not the kind that counted my faults.
But the kind that saw all my cracks and chose to stay
anyway.

I did not know then that the love I was searching for was
the love I needed to first give myself.

I was not weak.
I was scared.
I was still worthy of love.

Even broken, even lost — I was still worthy.
I just had not learned to believe it yet.

But then, something changed.

It was not a sudden thunderclap or a blazing revelation.
It was quieter than that.

A whisper against the wreckage I had become.
A small voice — maybe mine, maybe his — saying:
"You are still here. And that is enough."
I realized that waiting for someone else to love me the way
I longed for was a road without an end.

That healing did not mean stitching myself perfectly back
together to be chosen.
It meant choosing myself first, even with trembling hands.

I was tired of hiding.
Tired of shrinking.
Tired of believing I had to earn my worth.

And somewhere between the ache and the hope, I decided:
I would not live a life apologizing for my scars.
I would not ask permission to be loved anymore.

I would find my voice.

I would find my softness.

I would find myself again, not because someone else finally told me I was enough, but because I was ready to finally believe it myself.

Broken or whole, scared or brave —
I was still worthy.
I was always worthy.

The crowd remained silent, but it was not cold. It was holding her.

A woman clutched her shawl tighter. A man bowed his head. A child fidgeted—then stilled.

"I went back," she said. "To the place I buried the little girl I used to be. And I found her."

Her voice trembled—but it did not fall.

"She asked me why I left. I told her I did not know how to stay. And she forgave me."

"Today, I don't speak to be heard. I speak because I'm not hiding anymore."

A soft breeze stirred the willow's branches overhead, like a nod.

In the crowd, she saw Lina.

Daria's gaze locked with Lina's, and for a moment, the noise around them dissolved into a gentle, aching silence.

A forgotten memory stirred inside Daria — the scent of wildflowers, the sound of giggling girls chasing the summer light through the village fields. She remembered a tiny hand reaching out to hers, years ago, belonging to a girl with wide, curious eyes and a braid always slipping loose, Lina.

They had been childhood companions once — not inseparable, but bound by a quiet understanding, the way two wildflowers might bend toward each other under the same sun. When Daria had fallen while climbing the orchard trees, it had been Lina who sat beside her without speaking, offering not words, but a single feather plucked from the grass, a silent promise that pain would pass, and lightness would return.

Seeing Lina now — grown, weathered by time, but still carrying a feather in her hand — felt like finding a secret note tucked inside the folds of her life, a note written long ago, and waiting for this very moment to be read.

Their eyes met, and in that meeting, Daria remembered not only who Lina had been, but who she had once been, too.

The girl with thoughtful eyes. Holding a feather in her hand.

Their eyes met. Something passed between them. Not yet a friendship, but a thread.

Daria placed her palm over her heart.

"If you're holding pain in silence… you're not alone, you're not broken. You're waiting to be seen."

She let the silence stretch. It did not press against her like before. It held her now, gently, patiently.

"I was told for so long that I was too much," she continued. "Too emotional. Too loud. Too sensitive. Too quiet. Too soft."

"I was told for so long that I was too much," she continued, her voice steady but carrying the tremor of old wounds.

"Too emotional — because I dared to feel everything, they tried so hard to bury.

Too loud — because my voice carried truths they did not want to hear.

Too sensitive — because I noticed the fractures in places, they wanted to look whole.

Too quiet — because sometimes I chose silence, and they mistook it for weakness.

Too soft — because I believed in healing more than in hardening, even when the world taught me to build walls."

She paused, her breath catching for a moment, before lifting her chin gently—not in anger, but in quiet strength.

"They told me I was too much because I reminded them of what they had forgotten:

How to feel,

How to listen,

How to be real.

And for a long time, I believed them.

I wore their labels like invisible chains.

But now I know,

I was never too much.

I was simply more than their fear could hold."

Her gaze swept across the faces.

"So, I learned to adjust. To disappear a little more each year. Until one day, I didn't recognize my reflection."

A man with gray at his temples looked down at his feet. A woman with a braid held her hand over her mouth.

Daria stepped further into the center; the willow was still behind her like a pillar.

"I lied to people who asked if I was okay. I smiled when I wanted to scream. I praised others so no one would notice I needed kindness, too." Which was not right.

"I didn't just abandon that little girl—I abandoned me."

The silence broke.

Not with noise. With presence.

One by one, they moved.

A woman placed a ribbon at the base of the willow. A boy took off a string from his wrist. An elder laid down a smooth black rock and whispered, "Thank you."

Daria stood among them, not above. Not apart. Just within.

She unfolded a cloth from her pocket, a stone etched with golden words:

"Even in the dark, you still belong to the light."

She placed it gently beside the others.

When she looked up, the little girl in the corner was standing now. Still barefoot. Still glowing.

Daria smiled.

Because she had not just spoken up. She had been heard.

Journal Entry 14: For Her Eyes Only

Today, I walked through a version of myself I did not know I was still carrying.

Not gently. Not elegantly, but with every step echoing, "This is yours. All of it."

I did not expect forgiveness. I did not expect clarity. I expected noise. Maybe resistance.

Instead, what do I find?

It was silence. Not the kind that avoids— the kind that accepts.

I think I have been standing at the door of that room in my heart for years. Touching the handle. Swearing, I will open it tomorrow. Telling myself, "You're not ready."

The truth is—I was never going to feel ready.

Therefore, I opened it anyway.

Moreover, behind that door… Was the version of me who still loved herself, even when everyone else forgot how?

There were parts of the past I thought I had buried. Turns out, I just hid them in prettier boxes.

Today, the lids came off.

Memories spilled everywhere—like feathers from a burst pillow.

Some were soft.

Some stung.

Some looked me in the face and said, "You pretended we didn't hurt you. But we did."

Was it true?

I finally said it back: "Yes. You did. And I lived anyway."

There is a line I thought of while sitting under the willow this evening: "I'm not trying to erase the past. I'm trying to stop letting it write the ending."

That is what today felt like. Like editing. Like taking the pen back from hands that did not deserve to write my name in their chapters.

I think I am learning that healing is not always about making peace.

Sometimes, it is about no longer needing an apology.

It is about walking past what broke you without having to explain why you are still limping.

On the other hand, ···

It is just sitting in the quiet and saying: "I'm still here. And that's enough."

Therefore, here is the truth I am closing today with:

I do not hate who I was. I do not hate who they made me become.

Moreover, I am in love with the version of me who finally looked back and whispered,

 "We made it."

Chapter 15: The Thread between Us

The village was quieter the next day.

Not empty—just still. Like a breath held between chapters. As if the earth had exhaled and was waiting to see what would rise next.

Daria sat beneath the willow, her back pressed gently to the bark. She had no offer today. No ritual. Just her breath and the thrum of her pulse synchronizing with the slow rhythm of the branches above her.

She was not waiting.

She was simply present.

The sound of footsteps approached—soft, hesitant. She did not turn to look. She already knew who it was.

Lina.

Still small in frame, but no longer uncertain in her steps.

The girl appeared at her side, holding the feather from yesterday. It fluttered slightly between her fingers like a secret trying to speak.

"I didn't know if you'd be here," Lina said.

"I didn't either," Daria replied.

Lina sat beside her without needing permission, as if the ground had saved her place.

"I've been thinking," Lina said after a while, "about what you said yesterday. And how I didn't know I needed it until I heard it."

Daria smiled softly. "Sometimes truth doesn't knock. It walks in and makes tea."

They sat in silence, rich and golden. Daria glanced at Lina's posture: curled inward, arms folded tight, eyes distant.

"I used to sit like that," Daria said.

Lina looked at her. "Like what?"

"Like I was trying to take up less space. Like being seen might undo me."

Lina nodded slowly, eyes misting. "That's exactly how it feels."

"I know," Daria whispered. "But you deserve to unfold."

Daria began to speak. Not in a monologue. In memory.

"My grandmother, Ana," she said, "moved through the world like the world was lucky to have her. Not loudly. She did not command attention. She drew it—like moonlight on still water."

For a moment, the crowd stood still, breathing her words in like air too pure to waste.

Then, quietly at first, a ripple moved through them. A low murmur of voices hushed but unmistakable, like leaves stirring before the wind rises.

They were not questioning her anymore. They were whispering about her courage — the kind of courage that did not shout to be heard, the kind that simply was. A strength woven into silence, anchored deeper than words.

"She speaks like one who has walked through fire," someone murmured from the right.

"She carries the ashes and the light," whispered another from the left.

"She's not trying to lead us," said an older voice, rough but awed. "She's trying to remind us how to lead ourselves."

The whispers grew, not in volume but in weight—layering over each other like a gathering tide, pulling the crowd into a slow, invisible current of awakening.

Some faces softened, eyes shimmering with something long buried. Some bowed their heads, not in defeat but in recognition — recognition of the part of themselves that Daria had dared to name, the part that still believed in healing, in rising, in the quiet, unbreakable strength of simply being present.

Lina's eyes widened.

"She taught me that our silence holds as much power as our voice—but that we must choose which to wield and when. That crying isn't weakness—it's sacred overflow."

She looked like the child she had once been — a happy little girl with wild curls bouncing in the wind, bright, untamed eyes, and laughter spilling out of her like sunlight.

Barefoot and fearless, she had run through meadows, believing the earth itself loved her, that every stone, every blade of grass, whispered her name.

She had chased butterflies just to greet them, sung to the rivers, and crowned herself with dandelions, never worrying about the bruises on her knees or the loudness of her dreams.

To her, every puddle was a secret portal, every cloud a ship bound for magical lands.

That little girl had carried a feather in her pocket, believing it could one day lift her into the sky.

She did not need permission to dance, to sing, to believe.

And now, after all the storms, all the forgetting, all the years of silence, that fearless, barefoot child had come back to her, not as a memory, but as a living part of herself she had finally found again.

They spoke until shadows stretched long over the grass. Until even the wind leaned in to listen.

Daria told stories about being too sensitive for some, too strange for others. About carrying shame like a second spine. About building herself, not from triumph, but from soft repetition—one moment of truth at a time.

Lina listened like someone receiving the blueprint for her becoming.

When Daria finally paused, Lina said quietly:

"I think my silence was a scream. I just didn't know anyone could hear it."

They walked the village path later, feather still in Lina's hand, and passed the elder's garden. She nodded at them but said nothing.

Not every echo is loud.

Some move like thread—stitching souls together before they realize they were ever apart.

That evening, Daria returned to the willow alone. She sat again, knees tucked, head resting lightly against the bark.

She closed her eyes, and in the silence, she imagined all the women she had ever been.

The loud one. The quiet one. The lost one. The glowing one. The one who screamed in silence and hoped someone would translate.

She closed her eyes, and in the stillness, she saw them — all the women she had ever been, gathering around her like quiet witnesses.

The loud one, who shouted her dreams into empty rooms, believing that volume could earn her a place at tables never meant for her. She had poured her truth into spaces that twisted it, and when she was broken, she thought it was because she was too much. She wished she had known that she did not need to raise her voice for those who were never listening. That real connection would have found her through presence, not noise.

The quiet one, who had learned to tuck her spirit into corners, mistaking invisibility for safety. She had been praised for being easy, agreeable, and silent— but her heart had wilted under the weight of unsaid words. She wished she had known that true quiet is sacred only when it is chosen, not when it is demanded by fear or guilt.

The lost one, who wandered through the wrong hands and hollow places, offering pieces of herself in the hope of being pieced together by someone else. She had worn masks stitched from others' expectations, and lost sight of the girl beneath. She wished she had known that belonging never requires betrayal of self — that real love sees you, not the mask you wear.

The glowing one, who had dared to shine so brightly that even the shadows whispered of her, only to be asked— quietly, cruelly—to dim herself to be loved. She had smothered her flame to comfort those afraid of light. She wished she had known that her glow was not arrogance. It was her map, her birthright, her offering to a world starving for truth, the one who screamed in silence — the girl who carried oceans inside her chest, praying that someone would hear the waves crashing against her ribs. She had waited for a rescuer, someone to decode the language of her pain. She wished she had known that her voice, however trembling, was already fluent in worth. That she did not need to be rescued — she only needed to be heard by herself first.

All of them — the fierce, the quiet, the lost, the brilliant, the aching — were her. Not mistakes. Not failures. Only stages of becoming.

And now, barefoot in the light of her own making, she gathered every one of them — held their faces in her hands, forgave their fears, blessed their hopes — and walked forward.

Carrying them all home.

Home to herself.

They all sat beside her now.

And together, they whispered:

"We forgive you. Thank you for coming home."

Journal Entry 15: For Her Eyes Only

Today, I did not just speak.

I remembered. Not with words, but with presence.

There was no script. No performance. Just two women sitting beneath a willow and sharing the silence between their scars.

Lina looked at me as if she had been waiting for her whole life to be told she did not have to disappear. I knew that look. Because I wore it for years.

We talked about grandmothers. About women who moved like prayers, no one knew how to answer. Mine smelled like thyme and old stories. Hers, I think, still lives in the way Lina hesitates before saying her truth aloud.

I told her something Ana once told me:

"There's strength in tears, there is wisdom in waiting, and the ache you carry isn't weakness. It is proof you feel deeply enough to change things."

Lina cried.

So, did I.

It did not feel like breaking. It felt like opening.

There is something holy about being seen without being fixed.

Lina did not ask for answers. She just asked if she was allowed to speak. I said yes, not because I had permission to give…and only because no one ever told me I could when I was she.

I thought silence kept me safe. It did not. It just made me invisible in rooms I never deserved to vanish from.

I am starting to believe that softness is a language, and that women like us have always spoken it—quietly, with our hands, our lullabies, and our ability to hold others even when we are breaking.

We are not made to be loud. *We are made to be real.* To breathe through pain without needing to perform our survival.

Today, I did not feel like a healer or a prophet or anything grand.

I felt like a mirror. As I was finally showing someone what I once needed to see: A woman who did not flinch at her own truth.

Now, for the first time, I was not ashamed of my gentleness. I did not apologize for not being "tougher."

I let my voice shake. I let my story unfold in pieces. Somehow, it was enough.

Before she left, Lina said,

"You remind me of the person I thought I lost."

And I wanted to say, "That's because I've spent my whole life trying to find her too."

The world does not always listen to women who speak gently. Maybe that is the point. We are not here to be heard by everyone.

We are here to speak for us, the ones who have been waiting in the quiet. The ones who thought they were alone in their softness. The ones who carry feathers instead of swords.

If you find this page, I hope it feels like someone took your hand.

I hope it reminds you:

Even in the dark, you still belong to the light.

Chapter 16: The Echoes She Carried

Lina's voice cracked halfway through the story. Not because it broke her, but because it finally did not.

Daria sat beside her on the edge of the village square, not speaking. The wind moved gently between them, like breath between thoughts.

"She made me clean the same spot over and over again," Lina, whispered. "Not because it was dirty. Because she wanted to control something."

Daria did not move.

"She wasn't cruel," Lina added, softer. "Just... terrified of mess. Of grief. Of being left again."

They watched two children chase a stray ribbon across the road.

"She cried once," Lina said. "When I dropped a bowl. It did not even break. But she cried like it was the end of everything."

Daria nodded slowly. "Some things don't need to shatter to remind us we're holding too much."

Back beneath the willow, they sat again that night. Lina placed the feather in her lap, smoothing it like a fragile truth. Daria lit a small candle. No wind touched it. Not tonight.

"Do you think they know?" Lina asked.

"Who?"

"The villagers. About... us. About what we carry."

Daria touched the bark of the willow. "I think they do. But maybe they didn't know how to say it."

Lina pulled out a folded paper and handed it to Daria.

"They're writing now," she said. "Like the feather gave them permission."

Daria opened it slowly.

It read: "She made me remember what I promised myself I'd forget. And I think... that's why I'm not angry."

The next day, they gathered in the village center.

No drums. No speeches. Just eyes wide open.

One by one, villagers walked forward with their tokens—
small objects tied to meaning.

A red thread. A carved stone. A single button.

Each one was placed at the base of the willow. Each one
carried like a whisper of something unfinished.

Lina stood up. Her voice was slow but steady.

"We've been waiting for permission to speak. But maybe we
needed permission to feel."

Silence. No one interrupted.

"I used to be afraid of my own story," she said. "Now I
understand... it wasn't just mine. It was part of ours."

Daria stepped forward, too. She did not raise her voice. She
did not quote anything profound.

She simply said:

"You are not the only one who's ever been afraid to begin."

Then she walked. Not away, but through them:

They all parted—not out of reverence, but recognition.

At sunset, Lina reached into her pouch and gave Daria one
last folded scrap. It was written in a rushed, scribbled hand:

"Because of her, I opened the window this morning."

And for Daria, that one... That one was everything.

Journal Entry 16: For Her Eyes Only

Lina spoke today. Not to impress. Not to be brave. Just... because it was time.

And when she did, I saw it— she had become the voice I once searched for.

Her story unfolded slowly. Not like speech. Like a wound that finally exhaled.

She told me things that made my memories shift inside me, like puzzle pieces trying to remember where they belonged.

She spoke about absence. About the kind of silence that does not feel peaceful, it feels like punishment. She told me how her mother's grief turned into rules, and how her childhood was made of clean spaces and shut mouths.

I thought:

We all had mothers like that, became mothers like that, or survived them.

Then she did something I did not expect. She shared the village's grief. Notes. Scraps. Crumpled pieces of paper with trembling handwriting and hearts that had been quiet for too long.

It was not just Lina telling her story.

It was the collective ache of people who had never had the words.

Ilena, the shawl-maker, who had not cried since her son left. Tomas, the elder, who forgot the sound of his mother's voice until he heard mine. The boy with no name dreamed of birds after seeing one painted in the clearing.

They came through Lina. And I listened.

Not with pity. Not with answers. With the kind of reverence you give to a sunrise that shows up after too many storms.

I have been telling myself for so long that I had to be the first voice. The loudest. The fearless one.

On the other hand, maybe… maybe the bravest thing is to let others speak, too.

Maybe the mark of healing is not how well I perform being whole. It is how gently I make space for others to arrive unfinished.

And they did arrive today! One by one. No confetti. No declarations. Just offerings.

Ribbons. Stones. Memories. Laid at the base of a tree that never once asked to be worshipped—just witnessed.

I looked around and realized something wild: I am not carrying their stories. They are carrying each other now.

And me!?

I am not the fire. I am not the cure. I am not the center.

I am the open door.

The soft circle where silence becomes something sacred. Not erasure. Not escape.

Home.

Lina held my hand like it was a lifeline, but I knew in that moment… she did not need me.

She chose me.

And that, somehow, felt better than being needed.

So if anyone ever finds this page, let it be proof that the quiet ones are not empty.

They are just learning to echo.

Chapter 17: The Weight of Becoming Light

The village had gathered again.

Not with ceremony. Not with urgency, but with that kind of stillness that means something sacred is about to begin.

The willow stood at the center, quiet as always, listening.

Daria stood beneath it. Not above anyone. Not on a pedestal. Just... present.

Lina stood nearby, her ribbon now tied into her braid, a small smile on her lips. Her eyes glimmered—not just with tears, but also with something brighter. Recognition. Readiness.

The villagers formed a wide circle—men and women, children and elders, those who had once turned away, and those who had always watched from the shadows.

Daria breathed in. The air was cool and bright. Her heart was not racing. It was steady.

This was not a speech. It was a return.

She stepped forward.

"There is a kind of pain no one sees," she began, her voice gentle. "It doesn't scream. It folds itself into how we walk, how we laugh, how we stay quiet in moments we should speak."

She let the silence breathe.

"I know that pain. I carried it for years like it was a part of my name."

A soft breeze moved through the trees, as if exhaling.

"People will tell you transformation looks like fire—fast and beautiful, only they forget the truth. Transformation is slow. It is quiet. It is soft. It looks like getting up on a day you wanted to stay hidden. It sounds like saying 'I don't know' and meaning it."

She looked at the crowd, not for approval, but with invitation.

"You don't heal all at once. You do not find yourself fully formed. You gather. A piece here. A truth there. A moment where you finally cried. A day where you finally laughed again."

Her hand lifted and pressed gently over her heart.

"You don't need to be ready to begin. You just need to be honest."

A murmur passed through the circle. Not noise—acknowledgment.

"And sometimes... the most radical thing you can do is say no."

She paused, her eyes sweeping across the faces.

"No, I will not carry what doesn't belong to me.

No, I will not keep shrinking to fit someone else's comfort. No, I will not pretend I am not in pain.

No, I will not apologize for my softness, my voice, my tears, and my fire."

Her voice did not rise, it deepened—like roots in soil.

"You are not too much. You never were. You were just too true for a world that forgot how to listen."

Someone in the crowd placed a hand over their chest. Another quietly wiped a cheek.

"They told me to harden, but I stayed soft. They told me to forget, but I remembered. They told me to be smaller. But I returned to my full shape!"

She opened her hands as if releasing an old weight into the wind.

"Feather by feather, I came back to myself. And so can you."

A small boy stepped forward, holding a painted feather. He knelt and placed it at the base of the willow with the kind of reverence children are born knowing.

Daria knelt and touched it gently.

"Transformation doesn't demand perfection. It asks for presence. Not all at once, but step-by-step. Breath by breath. Feather by feather."

She rose slowly. Her eyes moved across the circle. Some were crying. Some were simply still. All were listening.

"If something doesn't fit your soul, you don't owe it your loyalty. If someone cannot meet you in your truth, that does not make your truth too loud. If your voice shakes, speak anyway. If you feel alone, look again. We are all here."

She spread her arms—not wide, just open.

"I am not asking you to be fearless. I am asking you to be honest. I am not asking you to rise all at once. I am asking you to rise with care. For yourself. For the one you used to be. For the one still becoming." She stepped closer to the center of the circle. A hush fell deeper, like even the trees leaned in.

"Let this place be your beginning. Let this be where you whisper to yourself: I am still here. I am still worth showing up for. And I will not disappear again."

Her voice softened to a whisper.

"Feather by feather, you will return, and when you do, you will see... You were never broken. You were always becoming."

She closed her eyes, and the willow behind her shifted—subtle, swaying—as though bowing in the wind.

Then she opened her arms, wide now, and lifted her chin.

"Come with me. Not because I have all the answers, but because I know how it feels to ask the questions. And not be afraid of the silence that follows."

And something remarkable happened: The villagers stepped forward.

Quietly. Reverently.

Each carried something—feathers, notes, stones, and torn scraps of grief made into offerings. One by one, they placed them at the base of the willow. Each one a sentence of a story they had not known how to speak—until now,

And Lina was at her side. Still. Unwavering.

The crowd started whispering, and Daria turned, not to stand above, but to walk among them.

She stepped beside an elder woman who carried a locket with no chain. Daria reached out and held her weathered hands.

She knelt beside a man who had not spoken in two seasons. Together, they watched his tears fall like offerings.

She took the hand of a child whose shirt bore a stitched star and whispered, "You're not too small to matter."

To each person, she offered no solutions. Only presence.

Only truth.

Only space.

Then, from the farthest edge of the circle, a voice rose.

Not loud.

Not confident.

Just true.

"Feather by feather."

Then another, and another.

Until the whole village was whispering it. Feather by feather! Feather by feather! Feather by feather!

It echoed, not in volume, but in gravity.

Nothing shook. Yet it changed everything.

Daria closed her eyes. A single tear slipped down her cheek.

Not grief. Not pain.

Gratitude.

She turned to the willow. Her hand pressed gently to its bark.

"You don't have to wait for the right day," she said. "Or the perfect version of yourself. You can begin today. Even if you are trembling. Even if you feel like a mess. You can begin now."

She looked at them all—each face a chapter, each silence a sentence.

"This is not about becoming someone new. This is about remembering who you have always been. Beneath the fear. Beneath the forgetting."

She knelt. Placed her palm on the earth. And whispered:

"Let this be the ground where your healing takes root."

She stood again and lifted her gaze.

"This is my final invitation: Come with me. BE YOU. Not because I have arrived, but because I am walking, and I want you to walk beside me. We do not need to know the destination. We just need to begin."

Then, softly, silently, a single silver leaf fell from the willow.

It landed at her feet.

A gift. A promise. A beginning.

Journal Entry 17: For Her Eyes Only

Feather by Feather!

I did not plan to change anyone.

I only meant to come home to myself. To stop hiding. To stop apologizing for being too much and too little all at once. To peel back the silence that had grown around me like bark, thick and brittle. To look at the girl I used to be and whisper, "I remember you now."

But when I spoke... they listened.

Not the way people listen to noise. They listened as if they were remembering something inside themselves. As if my voice had echoed into a place they had boarded shut, and in their listening, something cracked— not in me, but in them.

And that is when I knew.

This was never just about me. My story was never meant to stay behind my ribs.

It was a door.

When I opened it, they walked through.

I saw it happen, in real time. The shift. The unfreezing.

The way someone blinked too long because tears were catching in a place they did not know still felt. The way hands fidgeted with sleeves, hair, and rings— not from nerves, but from recognition. The way no one interrupted the silence between my words, because they knew. That silence was sacred.

I did not plan to lead. I did not want to be anyone's lighthouse. I was still learning how to hold my flame.

However, sometimes, when you rise, you carry others with you. Not on your shoulders— but in your light.

I used to think becoming meant rising out of the ashes like something polished. Something impressive. Now I know—

Becoming is not fire; It is returning. Slowly. Softly. Feather by feather.

Lina stood beside me today like a memory that had been waiting to arrive. I saw in her what I had once begged someone to see in me. Not potential. Not promise. Just presence.

She did not need fixing. She needed to witness.

And in the way she looked at me—eyes brimming, voice trembling—I felt it:

I was not the only one.

None of us is.

We have all broken quietly. We have all whispered our truth into the dark and hoped the night was kind enough to hold it. We have all believed, at some point, that we were too lost to be found again.

Yet, here we are:

Still standing. Still soft. Still becoming.

They came forward—those villagers, those strangers, those pieces of myself I had not known were walking around in other bodies. Each one carried something: a ribbon, a stone, a word they had never said aloud. Moreover, they placed it at the foot of the willow, not to be forgotten… But to be seen.

And I stood there, not tall. Not grand. Just true.

I thought this is how change happens. Not in revolutions. In remembrance.

What I feel now… is not joy.

It is something quieter. Something steadier.

Peace.

Peace that hums beneath the bones. Peace that does not ask for applause. Peace that says:

I do not need to perform to be whole.

I used to want to be saved. Then I wanted to save everyone else.

Now?

I just want to be here.

Breathing. Listening. Existing in the fullness of who I have always been beneath the noise.

Because this version of me—the one who stood under the willow and spoke with her whole heart— she is not someone new.

She is someone I have been remembering… feather by feather.

When I was younger, I thought healing meant erasing scars. Now I know healing means wearing them openly. Not as wounds, but as proof.

Proof that I survived. Proof that I returned. Proof that I kept breathing through every moment that tried to astound me.

There is nothing tidy about healing. There is nothing cinematic. It is raw, boring, beautiful, and lonely. Moreover, full.

Sometimes it looks like a journal. Sometimes it looks like weeping into the dirt. Sometimes it looks like letting someone see you when you do not have answers, just tears and trembling, and truth.

Sometimes it is just waking up and choosing to try again, and again, and again.

The girl I used to be?

She is still here. Not haunting me, but holding me!

She walks with me now. We are not fighting anymore. We are one breath, one body, one story.

If she could speak right now, I think she would say:

"Thank you for remembering. Thank you for not abandoning me forever. Thank you for building a life where we both belong."

I used to whisper my pain like a secret. Now I speak it like a spell.

Because maybe the most sacred thing we can do... is speak ourselves back into being.

Feather by feather. Word by word. Breathe by breath.

I am not loud; nevertheless, I am not silent.

I am not healed, but I am whole.

I am not waiting. I am walking.

What I know is…

The path ahead of me is not certain, but it is mine.

If anyone ever finds this page, let it be proof:

You do not have to be brave to begin. You just have to be honest.

You do not have to wait for someone to hand you permission. You already have it.

You do not have to know who you are yet. Just begin where it aches.

Begin where it softens. Begin where it remembers.

AND if you're scared? Good. That means your heart is still awake.

Walk anyway.

Speak anyway.

Return anyway,

And when you do—when you take that first trembling step back to yourself— I WILL BE HERE:

Not ahead. Not behind,

JUST BESIDE YOU!

Feather by feather. Always.

PART 2- RETURN

Chapter 18- The Call Home

The sun hung low when Daria returned to the village — a softened gold spilling across the cobbled streets, the worn rooftops, the familiar bends of the road she had once known better than her reflection.

She walked slowly, barefoot, her steps touching the ground with reverence, as if the earth itself were a memory she was trying to remember fully. The scent of wood smoke and ripening fields filled the air. Somewhere, a door creaked open and closed. A child's laughter floated from the far end of the lane, brief as a bird's song.

They saw her.

From windows half-shuttered, from doorways half-opened, the villagers watched — silently, uncertainly — as if unsure whether to believe in the woman who had left as a girl and returned as something they could not name.

Daria did not wave. She did not smile too brightly or shrink herself to make the space more comfortable. She simply walked, carrying herself the way the trees carried the wind — quietly, without permission.

Some faces she recognized instantly. Others had blurred into the years, changed by grief or age or stubbornness.

But she felt it — the weight behind their eyes. Curiosity. Hope. Resentment. Fear.

And under it all, something deeper still — a tired kind of longing, buried so long it almost didn't know how to reach the surface anymore.

She carried no luggage. No explanations. No apologies.

Only presence. And presence, she knew now, was more powerful than any speech she could have prepared.

The village was the same — and not. The buildings leaned a little more. The square felt smaller. The trees in the fields had grown wilder, their branches thicker, untamed.

She slowed as she approached the small stone square at the heart of the village — a place that had once seemed so vast when she was a child. Now it looked almost fragile, as if time had been gently wearing it down grain by grain, breath by breath.

The fountain at its center still stood, though the water no longer ran. Cracks ran like delicate veins along their sides, moss-curling green against their base.

Once, she had danced around it with wild, laughing feet — a girl who believed the world was infinite.

In the corner of the square, the old bench remained — half-swallowed by weeds, the paint peeling back in long curls like sunburned skin.

Daria moved toward it, her steps slow, deliberate, each footfall a conversation with the earth she had once abandoned.

When she sat down, the wood creaked beneath her weight, not in protest, but in recognition.

She looked out over the square, and for a moment, she could almost see them — the girls they had all once been.

And she wondered — had the village changed? Or had she?

Maybe it did not matter.

Maybe it was enough that she had returned with eyes that could finally see the beauty she once overlooked, and the strength in the cracks she had once despised.

Daria closed her eyes, feeling the late sun kissing her face, and breathed in the ancient pulse of the place that had made her, broken her, and now, if she allowed it, could help heal her.

She opened her eyes, and across the square, she saw a figure.

Standing half in shadow, half in light — Lina.

Their eyes met across the distance. Neither moved at first. The space between them stretched taut like a thread spun from memory and all the words left unsaid.

Daria stayed seated on the bench, allowing the moment to unfold without rushing to fill it.

When Lina reached her, she stood in silence. Daria moved over, making room on the bench. A simple gesture — an offering without demands.

For a moment, Lina hesitated. Then, with a breath that seemed to cost her something, she sat.

Not too close. Not too far. Just enough.

The evening settled around them, golden and kind.

After a long while, Daria rose from the bench, brushing the dust from the back of her skirt. Lina stood too, a little slower, as if unsure whether the spell of the moment would break if she moved too quickly.

They did not speak as they crossed the square together. They did not need to.

The village unfolded around them — the worn paths, the cracked shutters, the gardens tangled with late summer vines. Everything carried the fingerprints of time and survival — imperfect, enduring.

They passed the old bakery, its windows fogged from the day's work. Daria caught a glimpse of the baker's daughter — now a woman — arranging loaves behind the counter. She looked up briefly, their eyes meeting for a fraction of a second, before she turned away, pretending not to see.

They passed the smith's workshop next — the smell of hot iron thick in the air. The blacksmith's grandson hammered something unseen behind the open door, each strike ringing out like a heartbeat against the fading light.

Lina spoke softly. "Sometimes I wonder if they even know how much they're still hurting. They hide it so well, even from themselves."

Daria nodded. "It's easier to pretend the cracks aren't there. But eventually... they show. In anger. In distance. In silence."

They turned onto a narrower street, where ivy curled hungrily over the stonewalls, where once Daria and Lina had raced each other barefoot, laughing until they fell gasping into the grass.

"Do you ever think about it?" Daria asked. "The girl you used to be?"

Lina laughed softly. "All the time. She is still inside me somewhere. Smaller. Quieter. But she's there."

Daria smiled. "Maybe that's why we're here. To remember her. To bring her home."

They walked past the houses that had once held every certainty and every wound. The doors were closed, but Daria could feel the people inside — stirring, noticing, wondering.

At Lina's small, whitewashed home near the edge of the village, they entered quietly.

Inside, the air smelled of wood smoke, old books, and something sweet. A rough wooden table stood at the center, surrounded by mismatched chairs. A kettle hissed softly on the stove.

Lina poured them tea in chipped mugs. No words were needed yet. They sipped in the heavy silence of old pain and cautious hope.

"You could stay," Lina said eventually, voice barely above a whisper.

Daria stared into the dark liquid swirling in her cup.

Stay.

The word echoed inside her — not a chain, but an invitation.

"I think I'd like that," she said, her voice steady and clear.

Later that night, long after the village had tucked itself into sleep, Daria stepped outside.

The stars stretched overhead, endless and tender. She stood barefoot on the worn stone step, breathing in the cool, ancient air.

Above her, the sky shimmered — the same sky she had once prayed to as a girl. But she no longer begged it to carry her away.

She no longer looked for rescue.

She tilted her face upward, feeling the immense quiet of belonging settle deep in her chest.

Somewhere in the darkness, an owl called out — a low, patient song.

Daria smiled and whispered to the waiting night, to herself, to everything she could not see but now trusted completely:

"I'm here. I'm staying."

And somewhere deep inside, a new root took hold — strong, unshakable, and free.

Chapter 19- The Echoes Within

The days unfolded like quiet petals — slow, cautious, almost shy.

Daria stayed. She woke each morning before the village stirred, feeling the hush of the fields, the first breath of mist curling between the trees. She slept under the same roof each night, the stars pressing against the windows like ancient witnesses.

And slowly, almost imperceptibly, the village began to shift around her.

It was not in grand gestures or sweeping declarations. It was in the way Mrs. Eberly, who once crossed the street to avoid her, now lingered a heartbeat longer when their paths met. It was in the way the children, who first watched her from behind fences, now left chalk drawings on the stones where they knew she would pass. It was in the way Lina, wordless but steady, remained nearby.

Presence, Daria had learned, was a language all its own.

You did not have to shout to be heard by those ready to listen. You did not have to demand to be seen by those whose hearts had begun to remember how to look.

She walked the familiar roads with quiet feet and open hands, and the village, in its stumbling, wounded way, began to walk toward her.

Not all at once. Not completely. But enough.

The morning stretched wide and pale when Daria stepped out into the waking village.

She carried no agenda. No grand mission.

Only herself — quiet, listening, present.

The dirt path beneath her bare feet was cool and familiar, worn smoothly by decades of footsteps. The scent of damp earth rose with the mist, curling into the folds of her dress, threading through her hair.

At the edge of the square, near the crumbling chapel where prayers had once been stitched into stone, she saw her:

Mrs. Arlin.

Bent over a patch of stubborn weeds, hands roughened by years of unspoken grief, shoulders sagging under weights no one spoke of.

Daria hesitated.

In another life — the girl she had once been — she would have rushed forward, babbling kindness, offering help like a banner to be waved.

Now she knew better.

Healing did not come from force. It came from offering a presence strong enough to hold silence.

She approached slowly, each step a whisper of permission rather than intrusion.

Mrs. Arlin looked up sharply when Daria's shadow brushed the edge of her garden.

Her face was a map of storms — lined with sorrow, weathered by years that had stolen more than they had given.

For a moment, neither spoke.

Daria did not fill it.

She only knelt, slowly, onto the damp earth nearby — not too close, not too far — and began pulling weeds alongside her.

No words.

Just the soft, steady work of hands in the soil.

After a long while, so long the mist had begun to lift, and the sun had begun to lace gold across the rooftops — Mrs. Arlin spoke.

"They said you would never come back," she said, her voice low and almost breaking. "They said you had forgotten us."

Daria's fingers curled around the root of a stubborn thistle. She pulled gently, feeling it resist, feeling the earth's reluctant surrender.

"I never forgot," she said softly, without defense. "I just needed to remember myself first."

Mrs. Arlin grunted — a sound that was neither approval nor anger. Perhaps just exhaustion.

Another silence stretched.

Then, almost under her breath, as if it hurt to admit it, Mrs. Arlin said, "My boy used to run these fields with you."

Daria closed her eyes for a moment, the memory flooding back — small feet pounding the earth, laughter ringing wild and free, a boy with eyes the color of river stones.

"I remember," she said, her voice catching on the sharp edges of the past.

Mrs. Arlin's hands stilled.

128

"He is gone now," she said simply.

Daria did not offer empty condolences. She did not try to fill the space with false hope.

She only nodded once, deeply, and reached over, pressing a single hand to Mrs. Arlin's rough, worn one.

No words could stitch a loss like that closed. But touch. Touch could say, I see you. I remember too. You are not alone.

Mrs. Arlin did not pull away.

They sat there, bent over the earth, breathing the same broken, beautiful air.

The sun climbed higher, lighting the spaces between the leaves.

And somewhere inside that moment, a crack opened. A small, silent healing began.

Not perfect. Not whole.

But enough.

When Daria rose from the garden, she walked toward the old village well. There, perched on the crumbling wall, was a boy.

No more than twelve or thirteen, swinging his legs and tracing invisible shapes in the dust.

Their eyes met.

"You are her, right?" he asked. "The one who left?"

"Yes," Daria said simply.

The boy grinned.

"You look different. Like you have seen things."

"I have seen many things," she said. "And felt even more."

He leaned forward eagerly.

"Will you tell us?"

"Maybe," she said. "If you listen with your heart."

The boy nodded solemnly.

"I can do that."

Daria smiled and touched his shoulder lightly before walking on.

At Lina's home, the evening was thick with the scent of tea and wood smoke.

They sat across from each other at the old table.

"I used to think staying meant failure," Lina confessed.

Daria listened.

"But maybe wanting more does not always mean running away," Lina continued.

Daria reached across the table and placed her hand gently over Lina's.

"Sometimes wanting more means having the courage to stay. To love what is broken."

They sat together, the silence between them deep and good.

Later, Daria wandered to the fields at twilight.

The world softened around her, the mist rising again like breath from the sleeping earth.

She walked familiar paths, the soles of her feet whispering against the ground that had shaped her.

In the distance, lanterns flickered to life in small windows, each one a tiny testament to endurance.

She understood now: Healing was not an explosion. Healing was an echo — a sound carried from one heart to another, a promise that presence could be enough.

The road curved gently before her, full of memories, full of new beginnings yet unseen.

And she kept walking, wrapped in twilight, wrapped in hope.

Later, Daria wandered to the old schoolhouse.

She laid her hand on the cracked door.

"I forgive you," she whispered — to the building, to the village, to the girl she had been.

The walls remained silent, but something shifted inside her — a soft, unseen release.

By the dry fountain, she found Old Thomlin.

"You look like your mother," he said.

"She stayed as long as she could," Daria replied.

He nodded slowly.

"I suppose we all did what we could."

Daria smiled, not in sadness but in honor.

That night, in Lina's house, Daria opened her journal and wrote:

*Tonight, I walked through the village of my past. Tonight, I touched the ghosts I once feared would swallow me whole. *

*But they did not devour me. *

*They greeted me like old, wounded friends — wary, cautious, but longing for recognition. *

*I saw the grief in Mrs. Arlin's hands. I heard the hunger in a boy's voice. I witnessed the brittle strength in Thomlin's bent frame. *

*Healing is not a lightning strike. Healing is an echo — a whisper carried from one soul to another, a presence that says, I see you. I remember you. You are not alone. *

*Tonight, I did not save anyone. I did not fix anything. *

*I only stayed. *

*I only listened. *

*I only loved. *

*And maybe—maybe that is enough. *

Outside, the stars spun silently overhead, and Daria, for the first time in a long time, felt ready to meet tomorrow.

Chapter 20- The Return

Daria walked slowly through the forest, the morning light filtering through the trees like golden whispers. Her fingers brushed the leaves as if they could speak, as if each one held a truth she had forgotten.

The ground beneath her felt alive, pulsing with the memories of those who had come before her—women who had carried burdens, secrets, and songs in equal measure. The path was not marked, yet she knew it.

Not with her mind, but with the part of her that had always known how to come home. She had not returned to be the same. She had returned because she was different.

Her cloak flowed behind her like a river, dark blue and embroidered with silver threads, which Lina had sewn for her. Every stitch was a prayer, a promise, a bond.

Daria remembered Lina's quiet hands, how they had trembled when she gave her the cloak.

"For when you walk back into the world," Lina had said, "but not as the girl who left."

Now, Daria walked not as the broken one, but as the one who had gathered her pieces. She walked with breath in her chest and questions in her hands.

Each tree she passed whispered a different name. Some were hers from childhood. Some were names she did not yet recognize.

Maybe they were names for who she would become. As she stepped past the edge of the trees, the first glimpse of the village emerged. Roofs she once hated. Windows, she once feared. Doors she once dreamed of fleeing from. Her breath caught—not from fear, but from the weight of memory. She closed her eyes.

"I am here," she whispered.

Not to the people, not to the world—but to herself, and that was enough. She took another step. Then another. The soil was soft beneath her boots. With every breath, something inside her settled. The crow cried overhead and flew east, toward the sun. Daria followed her footsteps softer than shadow, but heavier than ever before. She passed the orchard where she once fell and scraped her knees. Now, the apple trees were blooming, petals like stars drifting in the wind.

A young girl stood beneath one of them, watching her. Their eyes met. And for a moment, Daria saw her younger self. Not in a mirror, but in that child's face—brave, bruised, and bursting with dreams. The girl offered her an apple. Daria took it gently, whispered,

"Thank you, and the child ran off, disappearing behind a fence of lilacs.

The path curved gently, past the old well, where Daria once hid from her brothers during summer games. Now it stood in silence, worn by time, but still holding water.

She paused beside it, running her fingers along the stones. Her reflection shimmered in the surface, not the girl she once was, but a woman who had walked through shadow and fire and still carried light.

A breeze stirred, and she heard the soft hum of a familiar tune.

A lullaby.

Her mother's voice. Not real, but present. Echoing through her bones.

Voices drifted from a nearby garden—soft, indistinct, like memories she could not quite catch.

She followed them instinctively; her steps guided more by heart than reason. A wooden gate creaked open. On the porch of a familiar house sat an old woman in a faded shawl, shelling beans with methodical grace. Daria's breath hitched.

"Bunica… (Grandma)" The word escaped her lips like a prayer.

Though the woman was not her grandmother, the resemblance was strong enough to stir something deep within—something ancestral, something sacred.

The woman looked up. Her eyes, though aged, were piercing. Wise. Unafraid.

"I was wondering when you'd come," she said without surprise. "The willow spoke of your return."

Daria stepped closer, heart pounding.

"You remember me?"

"I remember the silence after you left. It echoed louder than any voice."

The woman stood, slowly but steadily, and opened her arms. Daria hesitated for only a second before falling into them. The embrace smelled of lavender, earth, and old stories. When they pulled apart, the woman motioned her inside.

"I kept something for you," she said, walking into the dim house. "Something your mother once gave me; in case you ever came back."

The small box was wrapped in a cloth embroidered with the same silver thread as Daria's cloak. She opened it slowly. Inside lay a single white feather, a folded letter, and a carved wooden charm in the shape of a spiral.

Daria touched the feather gently, and a strange warmth filled her chest. The letter read:

"If you are reading this, my daughter, then you've made the choice I always hoped you would, to return not to who you were, but to who you are becoming. This journey is not to erase the pain, but to remember the softness underneath it."

Tears welled in Daria's eyes. She felt her knees weaken and sat on the floor, cradling the box like a relic.

The woman placed a hand on her shoulder.

"Your mother left more than a letter. She left a legacy inside you."

The house grew still, as if the walls themselves were listening. Daria looked out the window. The village was no longer a place of fear. It was a map of everything she had overcome. She took the feather and tucked it into her braid.

One more step. One more piece returned to her.

She left the house as twilight crept across the sky. Lamps flickered in the distance. Someone played a song on a flute—soft, familiar, full of longing. As she walked back into the center of the village, people began to notice.

A child stared. An elder gasped. Someone whispered her name like a myth reborn.

But Daria did not falter. She carried herself like the river, shaped by every stone, but never stopped. When she reached the square, she stood still. The wind lifted her cloak, and the stars began to emerge above.

She did not need to be welcomed. She belonged.

And with that knowing in her bones, she whispered to the sky:

"Feather by feather, I have returned."

Then, as if the sky itself had heard her, a soft breeze rippled through the square, carrying petals from the trees and lifting them into a slow, spiral dance. The villagers gathered in quiet awe, as if witnessing a sacred rite.

No one spoke. No one moved.

From the edge of the crowd, Lina stepped forward. Daria turned. Their eyes met. And in Lina's gaze, there was no question, no doubt. Only love.

"Welcome home," Lina said, her voice like spring.

Daria exhaled, long and full. She reached for Lina's hand, and together they walked to the heart of the village—not to make speeches, not to explain, but simply to be. The willow tree near the fountain shimmered under the moonlight, and Daria knew she would return to it soon. There were stories to tell. There were names to remember. There were wings still to grow. And tomorrow, she will begin.

Feather by feather. ***

At dawn, the village awoke to birdsong and the smell of bread rising in the ovens. Daria stood on the hillside above the houses, barefoot in the dew, watching the light stretch like golden threads across the roofs. Her cloak lay folded beside her. Today she wore white. She returned to the fountain and laid a bundle of herbs and ribbon at its base. The children approached shyly, curiosity overtaking their hesitation. One of them, a girl with a tangle of curls and laughter in her eyes, reached for Daria's hand.

"Are you the feather lady?" she asked.

Daria smiled.

 "I am the one who listens. Do you have a story to tell?" The girl nodded.

The others sat cross-legged in a circle, waiting. Daria began, not with her own tale, but with theirs. She spoke of the willow that remembers. Of stars that leave notes in dreams. Of voices once lost that can be found again.

The village listened.

Later that afternoon, the elders invited her to the Hall of Stories, an ancient building made of stone and thatch, where the oldest memories of the village were guarded. Inside, the air smelled of beeswax and pine.

Daria knelt before them—three women and two men, each with hair silvered by time, eyes sharp with wisdom.

"We have watched you," one said. "We have waited."

Daria bowed her head. "I am ready." A bowl of mountain water was passed from hand to hand, and each elder placed their fingers in it before pressing them to Daria's forehead, chest, and palms.

"For remembrance," whispered the first.

"For courage," said the second.

"For truth," echoed the third.

"For forgiveness," came the fourth.

"For the seed of healing to bloom," concluded the last.

Then they began to hum, a vibration older than language.

Daria's body trembled, but she did not look away. By twilight, she emerged from the Hall renewed—wet with tears but glowing with something ancient and deep.

That night, as the stars stitched silver across the dark sky, she and Lina sat beside the fire on a small hill. Lina passed her a cup of wildflower tea.

"Do you feel different?"

"Yes," Daria answered honestly.

"But not like I changed. Like I remembered."

They sat in silence, listening to the fire crackle. Then Lina spoke. "I dreamed once that you would come back and bring the whole sky with you."

Daria leaned her head on Lina's shoulder. "And I dreamed of a place where the silence didn't hurt."

The stars blinked above them, and somewhere nearby, an owl called. Neither of them spoke again. They did not need to. The fire held their stories. And the night listened.

Feather by feather. ***

The following evening, the villagers gathered again in the square. A hush fell over the crowd as Daria stepped into the center, barefoot, holding a bundle of feathers tied with twine. The children sat in front, eyes wide, while the elders stood behind them, leaning gently on walking sticks that had seen more winters than most.

Lina stood at the edge, watching. The moon had risen full and golden, casting a soft light over the gathering.

Daria raised her hand, not to silence, but to welcome.

"I didn't return to be the same," she began, her voice clear and calm.

"I returned because I finally remembered who I am." She paused, the wind wrapping around her words.

"There were days I forgot the sound of my voice. Nights, I held silence like a shield. I carried shame like a second skin. But piece by piece, I began to remember. That I am not the things I lost. I am not what was done to me. I am the one who chose to rise."

She walked slowly as she spoke, meeting the eyes of the villagers one by one.

"I used to believe healing was a destination, a final place where pain no longer lived. Now I know—it is not a place. It is a rhythm. A breath. A small act repeated. A soft truth spoken. A door opened, even if only a crack."

She looked at the children.

"Your stories matter. Not when you are grown. Now. Your wounds are not shameful. They are sacred invitations to grow roots and wings at once."

She turned to the elders.

"And you, keepers of time and memory—you remind us how to sit with grief and laugh with ghosts. You are the bridge between what was and what can still be."

A single tear ran down her cheek.

"I came back not to save you, but to learn how to save myself with you. To remember that we do not mend alone. We mend in the warmth of the witness. In the tenderness of together." She knelt and placed the bundle of feathers at the center of the square.

"These are for the ones who didn't make it. The ones we lost in silence. To fear. To forget. Let us remember them every time we speak the truth. Every time we choose compassion."

The wind rose gently, swirling the feathers into the air like a dance of memory and grace, and Daria smiled through her tears.

"Feather by feather," she whispered again,

"We become whole." ***

Later that night, long after the fire had gone to embers and the square had emptied, Daria found herself walking toward the willow tree alone. The village slept behind her, wrapped in the safety of dreams. She knelt beneath the great tree, its branches like arms cradling her. The stars peeked between the leaves, and the hush of wind through its limbs reminded her of a lullaby she had never forgotten. She took out a small journal from the pocket of her cloak, the same one she had carried since the day she left.

Pages worn, some smudged with tears, others heavy with questions. She opened to a fresh page and began to write:

"Tonight, I remembered how it feels to be seen. To be part of something not because I was perfect, but because I returned. I thought the hardest part was leaving. But it wasn't. The hardest part was choosing to come back softer, and not bitter." "Tomorrow, I will speak with the council. Something new is stirring—not just in me, but in this land. I feel it. And maybe it's time we dream forward, not just backward."

She paused and drew a small spiral in the corner of the page, then whispered:

"Let this be the beginning of something brave."

She leaned back against the willow's trunk, letting her breath match the rhythm of the wind.

Chapter 21- The First Day of the After

Daria stood at the edge of the village square, facing the Hall of Stories once again, but this time not as a visitor. The air was still thick with anticipation. Word had spread—tonight, the council would gather, and they had asked for her.

She adjusted the collar of her cloak and looked down at her hands. They no longer trembled as they once did. They were steady now, not because the fear had vanished, but because she had learned how to carry it.

Lina found her by the fountain, a basket of herbs resting on her hip.

"They're expecting you," she said softly, brushing a strand of hair from Daria's cheek.

"I know," Daria answered in her voice, almost a whisper. "But I don't know what to say."

"You don't have to prepare speeches," Lina smiled. "Just bring the truth. That's all they've forgotten how to hear."

The Hall's wooden doors creaked open as the sun dipped behind the hills. Candles flickered inside, casting long shadows across the carved walls. Daria entered slowly, her footsteps echoing in the silence.

The five council members sat in a semicircle, each one a keeper of tradition, once strangers to her but now familiar souls who had listened during the feather ceremony.

Daria stood in the center, feeling the warmth of the willow

still within her chest.

"I didn't come here to lead," she began, "but I also didn't come to stay silent."

The elder with the raven pin on her shawl nodded. "Then speak, child of return. We are listening."
Daria took a breath.
"I believe something is changing—not just in me, but in this land, in this village. Something is growing again... and I think it is time we stop waiting for the past to return. Maybe it's time we begin to imagine a future."
Silence followed—not out of resistance, but reverence. Tonight was not for answers.
It was for the beginning.

The next morning, Daria returned to the council hall, not with speeches or demands, but with a satchel of folded parchment and a heart full of quiet fire.
The elders welcomed her again, their expressions curious.
"I couldn't sleep last night," she said, laying out the papers on the table. "Not because of worry, but because I saw something. Not a dream, not quite. A feeling. A map made of possibility."
She unfolded the parchments—sketched outlines of small gathering spaces shaded beneath trees, benches carved with the names of ancestors, a communal garden tended by children and elders alike. A small library where stories could be shared aloud. Circles, not podiums. Blankets, not thrones.

"It's not about building something new for the sake of change," Daria explained, her voice steady. "It's about remembering what we forgot. Listening. Healing together. Making space for the ones who never had a voice."

An older man with gnarled hands picked up a drawing of a willow-shaped storytelling pavilion. "This… this reminds me of my grandmother's house. She used to tell stories until her voice cracked with age."

"And maybe," Daria replied, "this will be the place where new voices rise, and old ones are honored."

The council did not nod immediately. But they didn't turn away either.

Lina entered quietly near the end, carrying a tray of bread and honey. She set it on the table without a word and took her seat beside Daria.

"Let's not call this a proposal," one of the elders said at last. "Let's call it a beginning."

Daria's hands relaxed.

The seeds had been planted.

Now, they would wait for rain.

It began quietly.

A woman named Mara came first. She had always sat in the last row during village gatherings, her shawl pulled tightly around her shoulders, her gaze fixed on the floor. She approached Daria near the well, hands trembling, voice no louder than a breath.

"I kept this," she said, unfolding a yellowed piece of paper.

"It's a letter I wrote to myself after my husband left. I never thought I'd show it to anyone."

Daria did not ask to read it. She simply placed her hand over Mara's and whispered, "Thank you for still carrying it."

Then came Emil, a boy of fifteen with ink-stained fingers and stories hidden in the margins of his schoolbooks. He handed Daria a stack of pages tied with twine.

"I write at night," he confessed. "So, no one will laugh. They're not real stories, just... feelings."

Daria took the pages as if they were sacred scripture. "They're real," she said. "Because you are."

Then there was Sorin, the oldest man in the village. He walked with a cane carved with symbols no one understood anymore. He carried a sealed envelope that he had written to his sister, who vanished during the famine.

"I never sent it," he said. "But if I read it aloud... would that be enough?"

Daria nodded. "More than enough."

That evening, the square filled again—this time not for ceremonies or plans. Just people sitting on blankets, under lanterns, holding papers, notebooks, letters, and trembling truths.

One by one, they rose. Voices cracked. Hands shook. The silence broke like thawed river ice, and something ancient stirred in the soil beneath their feet.

Stories had always lived here.

They had just waited for a place to land.

The gathering had ended, but Daria lingered by the willow tree, feeling the breath of night cool against her skin. Lanterns flickered low, and most villagers had returned to their homes, their hearts full but fragile.

That is when she saw her.

A young woman, no more than twenty, stood by the fountain, half-shrouded in shadow. She twisted the hem of her linen dress between her fingers, the tremor in her body visible even from a distance.

Daria approached slowly, careful not to startle her.

The girl looked up, eyes wide, brimming with words too long caged inside.

"I... I don't know how to begin," she stammered.

"You just did," Daria said gently.

The girl bit her lip, hesitated, then rushed forward, clutching Daria's hands as if they were the last rope before a fall.

"My name is Elina," she whispered. "And I've been silent for too long. I thought if I spoke, the world would crack open and swallow me."

Daria squeezed her hands. "Sometimes the world needs to crack a little so we can breathe again."

Elina's shoulders shook. She pressed a folded scrap of paper into Daria's palm—a confession, perhaps, or the first thread of her unraveling pain.

"I'm afraid," she said.

"That's all right," Daria replied. "You can be afraid. But

don't let it be the only voice you hear."

Tears slipped down Elina's cheeks, and Daria pulled her into an embrace beneath the shelter of the willow.

For a long moment, there were no speeches, no promises—only the sacred silence between two hearts daring to trust.

Above them, the branches swayed gently, carrying their first fragile hopes into the waiting sky.

The next morning, Daria sat by her window with the journal resting across her knees. The village had not yet woken; mist curled between the rooftops like quiet thoughts, and the birds still whispered instead of singing. She opened to a new page and let the pen move without force.

*"Last night, I saw what happens when one voice dares to rise—it stirs others. Not in grand waves, but like small ripples across a lake. Elina's hands trembled, but her truth was steady. That's what matters." *

"I always thought I had to carry the flame alone. But maybe I was never meant to be just a fire burning in solitude. Maybe I'm a torch meant to be passed, to light others, to remind them that their voices are not too small, too broken, and too late."

She paused, fingers tapping gently on the page, before writing the next line slowly, deliberately:

"I want to become the kind of presence that helps others become themselves."

There was no ceremony, no applause—only the quiet shift

of intention. But in that stillness, something powerful took root.

She closed the journal and exhaled.

Then stood, dressed, and stepped out into the rising day— not to lead, not to guide, but to walk beside.

The flame was no longer hers alone.

It belonged to the village.

It belonged to all who dared speak, even with a shaking voice.

It belonged to those who had not yet arrived.

It belongs to those who would stay behind and remember.

The village awakened slowly.

Children ran barefoot between garden rows while elders sipped morning tea beneath fig trees that had outlived generations, and in the center of it all, Daria stood with her palms turned upward, eyes closed, feeling the sun's first touch on her face.

Something was shifting. Not in a dramatic way—but in a gentle unfolding, like a letter being read for the first time.

People greeted one another differently now. With less suspicion. With softer eyes.

Elina walked by, nodding shyly. Mara joined the women baking bread and hummed a melody no one had heard from her lips in years. Emil sat in the shade of the storytelling tree, reading his words aloud to three curious boys.

Daria—she moved through it all not as a savior, but as a witness.

She no longer feared her voice. And she no longer felt responsible for carrying all the pain alone.

She met with Lina at the edge of the field where new shoots of mint and thyme had begun to sprout. They shared a silent smile, knowing no words could capture what had just begun.

That night, Daria lit a small candle in her window—not as a signal of sorrow, but as an offering to hope.

In her journal, she wrote only one line:

*"This is no longer just my story." *

Then she turned the page and left it blank—ready for others to fill it.

The first day of the after had begun.

Feather by feather.

Epilogue – The Quiet After the Echo

The willow stands tall.

Not as a monument to what happened, but as a companion to what continues. Daria walks the path often, not because she must, but because she *can*. Because the silence that once felt heavy now feels like space to breathe. The village, once wary of its own reflection, now sings softly with stories—not all of them loud, not all of them finished, but all of them *true*.

And Daria?

She no longer asks if she is ready. She no longer shrank to be loved. She no longer waits to be whole. She wakes up with the sunrise and greets herself with reverence. Some days, she still listens for doubt, but it whispers less and less.

Because now, she carries a feather in her pocket.

A reminder that softness is not weakness. That healing was never a race. That love—real love—begins inside. And sometimes, when the wind moves just right, she hears her own voice echo through the trees. Not the one that trembled. But the one that *stood tall* and said: **"I am still here. And I will not disappear again. **

This is not the end…

This is the soil where your roots can grow. Where your breath returns to your chest. Where your story begins— not with perfection— but with one truth…

**Feather by feather. ** --- **

As her journey was, so your journey begins, dear reader. ** You have walked through Daria's path with an open heart, and now it is your turn to take a step, not toward who you were told to be, but toward who you truly are.

YOU ARE LOVED,

YOU ARE STRONG,

YOU ARE READY,

YOU ARE BEAUTIFUL.

SO, WRITE YOUR STORY.

Whisper your truth. Break the shell. AND SHINE. *

*Because NOW ….IT IS YOUR TIME. **

For Her Eyes Only

Daria's Complete Journal

This journal holds the whispers of a journey too personal to be spoken aloud — thoughts written in silence, between the breaths of each chapter. Here, they unfold without interruption, feather by feather, like a trail of soft truths leading back to the soul.

What was once scattered across the pages of a life in motion is now gathered in one place — raw, unfiltered, and honest. These words belong to Daria, but they may also belong to you.

She wrote not to be heard but to feel. She poured what she could not say into ink—fleeting confessions, questions left unanswered, and prayers whispered through tears. This is not a polished story. It is the inside of a heart, written without performance or perfection. It is the language of healing before the healing has a name.

Some entries were written on days when the world felt too loud. Others on nights when silence wrapped around her like a forgotten blanket. Each carries a piece of the transformation that could not be seen from the outside.

Each one is a step — small, tender, and sometimes trembling — toward becoming.

If you are holding these pages now, you are meant to read them. Not with judgment. Not with logic. Only with the part of yourself that still believes in wonder. The part that dares to ask, 'Who am I, really?' and waits for the answer to arrive in whispers, not declarations.

This is Daria's journal. However, between the lines, you might just find your voice echoing back.

About the Author

Camelia writes for those learning to return to themselves—slowly, gently, and without apology. Her work is rooted in memory, healing, and the quiet magic that blooms when we stop asking for permission to feel. With a voice that listens as much as it speaks, she creates stories like invitations not to escape life, but to walk deeper into it.

She believes healing is not loud, it is honest. That softness is not a weakness, but a language. Those stories can be both mirrors and maps.

When not writing under her name, Camelia pens a whimsical series of children's books under the pen name Luna Night, where wonder is stitched into every sentence and magic is always just beneath the surface.

She lives somewhere between the roots and the wind, always listening, always becoming. Her words are not performance. They are a return.

HERE STARTS YOUR OWN JOURNEY

HERE STARTS YOUR OWN JOURNEY

HERE STARTS YOUR OWN JOURNEY

HERE STARTS YOUR OWN
JOURNEY

HERE STARTS YOUR OWN
JOURNEY

www.ingramcontent.com/pod-product-compliance
Lightning Source LLC
Chambersburg PA
CBHW070934250626
47159CB00009B/3250